Sev kissed her in a way he perhaps shouldn't if Naomi was going to keep her head.

Side on, eyes open for long enough to know what they were doing was breaking their rules.

Their legs were entwined, but now there was time for more. And so Naomi kissed him in a way perhaps *she* shouldn't. Three months of restraint had ended on the plane, but a different restraint ended this morning. She had never known a kiss like it. Their tongues swirled, mouths playing. She took in his lower lip just to feel it between hers; they stroked at each other's mouth, caressed the other's tongue. Yes, she had never known a kiss like it and, she guessed, after this morning she never again would.

Irresistible Russian Tycoons

Sexy, scandalous and impossible to resist!

Daniil, Sev, Nikolai and Roman have come a long way from the Russian orphanage they grew up in. These days, the four sexy tycoons dominate the world's stage—and are just as famed for their prowess between the sheets!

Untamed and untouched by emotion, can these ruthless men find women to redeem them?

You won't want to miss these sizzling Russians in this sensational quartet from *USA TODAY* bestselling author Carol Marinelli— available only from Harlequin Presents!

The Price of His Redemption

December 2015

The Cost of the Forbidden

January 2016

And watch for Nikolai and Roman's stories... coming soon!

Carol Marinelli

THE COST OF
THE FORBIDDEN

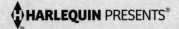

Recycling programs
for this product may
not exist in your area.

ISBN-13: 978-0-373-13400-7

The Cost of the Forbidden

First North American Publication 2016

Copyright © 2016 by Carol Marinelli

All rights reserved. Except for use in any review, the reproduction or utilization of this work in whole or in part in any form by any electronic, mechanical or other means, now known or hereinafter invented, including xerography, photocopying and recording, or in any information storage or retrieval system, is forbidden without the written permission of the publisher, Harlequin Enterprises Limited, 225 Duncan Mill Road, Don Mills, Ontario M3B 3K9, Canada.

This is a work of fiction. Names, characters, places and incidents are either the product of the author's imagination or are used fictitiously, and any resemblance to actual persons, living or dead, business establishments, events or locales is entirely coincidental.

This edition published by arrangement with Harlequin Books S.A.

For questions and comments about the quality of this book, please contact us at CustomerService@Harlequin.com.

® and TM are trademarks of Harlequin Enterprises Limited or its corporate affiliates. Trademarks indicated with ® are registered in the United States Patent and Trademark Office, the Canadian Intellectual Property Office and in other countries.

Printed in U.S.A.

www.Harlequin.com

Carol Marinelli is a Taurus, with Taurus rising, yet still thinks she is a secret Gemini. Originally from England, she now lives in Australia and is the single mother of three. Apart from her children, writing romance and the friendships forged along the way are her passion. She chooses to believe in a happy-ever-after for all and strives for that in her writing.

Books by Carol Marinelli

Harlequin Presents

The Playboy of Puerto Banus
Playing the Dutiful Wife
Heart of the Desert
Innocent Secretary...Accidentally Pregnant

Irresistible Russian Tycoons

The Price of His Redemption

Playboys of Sicily

Sicilian's Shock Proposal
His Sicilian Cinderella

The Chatsfield

Princess's Secret Baby

Alpha Heroes Meet Their Match

The Only Woman to Defy Him
More Precious than a Crown
Protecting the Desert Princess

Empire of the Sands

Banished to the Harem
Beholden to the Throne

The Secrets of Xanos

A Shameful Consequence
An Indecent Proposition

Visit the Author Profile page at Harlequin.com for more titles.

PROLOGUE

'YOU'RE ENGLISH?' NAOMI watched from the other side of a large polished desk as Sevastyan Derzhavin flicked through her résumé with little enthusiasm.

He'd already made up his mind that she hadn't got the job, Naomi decided. So it was now just a matter of going through the motions.

What she didn't know was Sevastyan never went through the motions.

Social niceties did not apply to him.

'I was born here and my father lives here in New York,' Naomi answered. 'So I'm legal…'

'I wasn't asking for that.' He shook his head 'I'm not really big on red tape. It was your accent that had me curious. How long have you been here?' He continued to look at her résumé and frowned as Naomi answered him.

'Twelve days.'

'You're staying in a hostel?' he checked.

'Just till I find somewhere to live, though that's proving harder than I thought it would.'

He glanced up and saw that she was blushing—she had been since the moment he'd called her name, or perhaps her complexion was just perpetually red?

'I thought that you said that your father lived—'

'His wife just had a new baby.' Naomi interrupted.

'I don't blame you, then.'

'Sorry?'

He stiffened.

It was the third time that she had said it.

'I don't blame you for not wanting to stay with him if there's a screaming baby.'

Naomi didn't respond but her slight swallow and blink told him that, very possibly, his comment was the wrong way around—that her father didn't want Naomi staying with him.

He had been about to tell her that they were wasting each other's time. Sevastyan didn't deal in emotion. Computers were his thing. Books too. Not people.

There was no point in dragging things out and so he would tell her that this wasn't going to work; that she could never be his PA.

And he would tell her why if she asked.

Naomi Johnson had one of those apologetic personalities that irked Sev.

One of the last English words he'd learnt had been 'sorry' and he rarely used it.

Naomi had said it twice even before taking her seat.

She had said sorry when he'd gone into Reception to call her in for the interview and she had knocked over her glass of water as she'd stood. Then, as she had taken a seat in his sumptuous Fifth Avenue office, he'd politely asked how her morning had been. Naomi clearly hadn't made out what he'd said and it had been 'sorry' again.

'It doesn't matter,' had been his irritated reply.

And now she had just said it again.

'I don't think it will work,' Sev said.

'Mr Derzhavin—'

'Sev,' he interrupted. 'I'm not a schoolteacher.' He looked up into serious brown eyes and, seeing her rapid blink, he reeled back a touch from his usual abrupt dismissal. She—Naomi—had clearly made a huge effort for the interview today. The hostel she was staying at was a dive yet she was here in a smart suit. It was a touch tight, Sev thought, noticing her curves. Her dark brown hair was neatly tied back and she looked…

Sev couldn't quite place it.

She reminded him of something, or rather someone.

He didn't really want to examine who or what it was, there was just, he decided, no need to be brutal.

'Look, Naomi, you're clearly qualified and for a twenty-five-year-old you have a lot of experience and you interview well but…' He watched her nervous swallow and found himself wanting to let her down gently. 'You've an extensive list of hobbies—reading, horse riding, ballet, theatre… It goes on. The thing is, the only hobby my PA can reasonably expect to have is me.'

'Felicity has already explained that to me,' Naomi said. Her first interview with his current PA had been thorough enough to leave Naomi in no doubt that the role would be a demanding one. Sevastyan Derzhavin's skills in cyber security were globally in demand. Apart from an impossible workload he was a rich playboy and had a little black book that was his PA's to juggle, along with his private jet and helicopter.

Yes, she had been told exactly what the role would entail. He was arrogant, emotionless, worked you to the bone but he paid through the nose for attention to duty.

Him.

From the bitter twist to Felicity's voice Naomi had soon guessed that there might be a more personal reason for the sudden vacancy.

'Even so.' Sev went to drop her résumé on his desk

and, Naomi was sure, terminate the interview and send her on her way.

'Would it help if I told you that I'd lied on my résumé?'

'Probably not.' Instead of standing, he leant back in his seat. 'Go on.'

'Well, I do like the ballet and theatre but it's stretching it to say that they're hobbies of mine and I haven't been on a horse since I was fourteen...'

'What about reading?'

'I'll read in bed.'

Sev opened his mouth to say something and then, very sensibly, he closed it.

God, he could so easily and so very inappropriately have responded to that. Clearly Miss Awkward had recognised the opening she had just given him because just as those full cheeks had been starting to pale, they had once again flushed pink the second she'd said it.

'Well, I can't command your time in the bedroom,' Sev said, and he hesitated again because, actually, he wouldn't mind doing just that...

He made a very abrupt verbal U-turn. 'I warn you—if I offered you the role then most of your waking hours would be devoted to me. Your time would be spent on a laptop, or the phone, sorting out *my* life. You wouldn't even have time to read your horoscope, it will be mine you turn to first.'

'I don't believe in them.'

'I bet you still read them, though?'

'Is that relevant?'

She was tougher than she had first looked.

Sev gave her an intense stare, barely noticing her full lips and round cheeks as her deep brown eyes drew him in.

And with that look Naomi revisited her need for the

role—twelve- to eighteen-hour days didn't trouble her, rather it was the company she'd be required to keep that did.

'I see you're engaged.' Sev glanced at the ring she wore before returning her solemn gaze.

'Again,' Naomi asked, 'is that relevant?'

'Actually, it is,' Sev tartly responded. 'Because you'd have to have the most understanding fiancé in the history of the world to put up with the demands that I would make on your time.'

'Well, my fiancé isn't here in New York with me, however…' Naomi hesitated for a moment and then decided that, no, if by some miracle he did offer her the role she wouldn't accept it anyway.

Twelve minutes ago her world had been complicated yet ordered.

Well, not ordered as such but twelve days ago she had arrived in New York.

Twelve minutes ago she had texted her father to suggest that they catch up for lunch after her interview.

She had just put her phone back in her bag and gone to take a drink of water when Sevastyan Derzhavin had walked out of his office and called her name.

'Naomi.'

He was beautiful.

Just that.

Dark haired, pale skinned, he had very long legs and despite the immaculate suit he looked as if he should be wandering out of a club or casino at 5:00 a.m. he was so rumpled and unshaven.

His tie was loosened, his grey-black eyes were a touch heavy lidded and he gave her not a smile as such, just a nod in the direction of his office and a vague, unrelated memory had popped into her head—she had remem-

bered the time she'd gone to see her lovely familiar female doctor for a pap and a sexy-as-hell locum doctor
had come out.

Naomi had flunked it and had asked the sexy doctor
for a flu injection instead. And she'd flunked it again as
Sevastyan had come out of his office and greeted her.
As she'd stood, she had got all flustered and knocked
over her drink. When he'd enquired, in a deep, Russian-
accented voice, about her day, she'd been so entranced
that she hadn't really heard what he'd said and he'd had
to repeat himself twice.

With every question he'd grown sexier.

With every vowel he uttered she wondered if the chair
she was sitting on might be battery operated. Somehow
even her list of hobbies had led them to bed and so now
all Naomi wanted to do was stand up and get the hell
out of there.

I'm an engaged woman, she wanted to say. *How dare
you make me feel like that?*

No, she didn't want the role.

'You don't speak a second language,' Sev checked.

'No.' Naomi shook her head. 'I don't.'

'At all?'

'Non,' Naomi said, and then laughed at her own fee-
ble joke.

He didn't laugh, just stared back at her.

'You know,' Sev finally said, 'the English are lazy.'

'Excuse me?'

'I mean the English-language-speaking world.'

'Oh.'

'They rely on others speaking their language.'

'How many languages do you speak?' Naomi asked
him.

'Five.'

Good, Naomi thought. She didn't have the job.

'Still, given that most everyone speaks English,' Sev said, 'I'm sure that we can work around it.'

Help.

'I just want to clarify that I'm only going to be in New York for a year,' Naomi said, giving him an out now and rather hoping that would be it, but he merely shrugged.

'You'd burn out long before then. I don't think I've ever had a PA last longer than six months. Three months…' He gauged. 'Yes, I think you would last about three months, though I'd hope for more.'

'Look…' Naomi flashed him a smile. 'I don't want to waste your time. Though your assistant was very clear that the hours were demanding I didn't realise that it would be quite so full on. I like my weekends…' She gave him another smile, which he didn't return. 'I'm actually here to get to know my father a little better and so—'

'You'd get weekends off.' Sev dismissed that obstacle. 'Unless we were overseas.'

'And also,' Naomi added, just to make certain that he didn't hire her, 'I don't really have experience in your field.'

'Experience in my field?' Sevastyan frowned and he knew exactly what she meant but he was enjoying watching her get flustered. 'I'm not a farmer.'

'I meant that I don't know much about cyber security.'

'If you did then you'd be my rival.'

She stood and held out her hand.

'I'm sorry, I—'

'Part of the package is an apartment overlooking Central Park. Well, once Felicity moves out. It's nice…' he mused. 'Well, I like living there.'

'We'd be in the same apartment block?'

It got worse and worse!

'It's huge. Don't worry, I shan't be knocking on your door to borrow a cup of sugar. It's convenient if there's an early morning or late-night meeting. And it saves time when we're travelling, which there's a lot of. Being in the same building shaves off ten minutes if I don't have to pick you up from another address and there's a helipad.' And then he told her what her wardrobe allowance would be, which should have had her cheering.

'No, really…'

Naomi wanted her life back.

She wanted a world where she had never seen this man. But Sev now wanted her.

She was as plump as forbidden fruit and, God, but he loved the word 'no'. He considered it a pesky firewall to get around or disable.

It really was a great motivator.

'Thank you for your time,' Naomi said, still holding out her hand, but he didn't offer his.

'Sorry,' she said again, only this time it didn't irk him. He simply sat in silence and watched her leave.

He picked up the next résumé and read through it.

Yawn, yawn, Sev thought, his mind still on the girl with the sad brown eyes.

Spaniel brown.

Like some puppy expecting to be kicked but hoping for love.

And a stray he did not need.

He headed out to call Emmanuel in.

The waiting room was empty.

'Felicity…' he called out to his PA, but her seat was empty too.

And her bag was gone.

There was her farewell message to him on the computer screen.

I FAKED IT!!!!

'No, you didn't.' Sev grinned but his smile faded as the lift opened and Emmanuel, presumably, dashed down the corridor.

'I'm so sorry that I'm late, Mr Derzhavin…'

Sev frowned. He recognised him. That's right, he had interviewed Emmanuel a couple of years before and now he was back for another go.

And he was five minutes late.

'Not the best first impression,' Sev said.

'I know but—'

'Let's not waste each other's time.'

'But…!'

Sev didn't wait to hear his excuses. Instead he headed back to his office and caught the last floral notes of Naomi Johnson. His mind made up, Sev picked up his phone.

Naomi was just checking hers when it rang and, given her recent text to her father, naturally she assumed it was him. He'd actually seemed impressed when Naomi had told him about the interview with Sevastyan. Maybe he was ringing to find out how it had gone?

'Hi, Dad, I was just—'

Her voice was all gushing and needy and not one she'd used on him, Sev thought. 'It's not your father. This is Sev.'

'Oh.'

He heard the sag of disappointment in her voice, which was a first for Sev—women were usually falling over themselves to get a call from him. 'Your boss.'

'Sorry?'

'Ha!' Sev said. 'We'll have to work on that one. Congratulations, Naomi, you've got the job.'

Naomi stood in the foyer and knew that she should end the call.

Simply hang up and get the hell out of there.

'I thought that I'd made it clear—' Naomi attempted, but Sev interrupted her.

'How about I sweeten the deal with quarterly trips home to the UK? I'm actually going there in November for a private visit. You can have a couple of weeks off. I'm sure your fiancé will be pleased to see you.'

Naomi swallowed but then frowned at his next question.

'Why didn't he come with you?'

'Excuse me?'

'To New York?' Sev said. 'Why did you come alone?'

'We trust each other...' Her voice was shrill because, bizarrely, at this very moment, Naomi didn't trust herself.

'I wasn't talking about trust, I'm just curious why he didn't come.'

Oh, he was like a shower of needles, getting into her skin. His question was one that Naomi had asked herself several times.

'He has an important job.'

'So do I,' Sev said, then he decided it didn't matter. A fiancé, and an absent one at that, was completely irrelevant to him so he deleted her fiancé from the file in his mind named Naomi Johnson.

Irrelevant.

'Come and work for me, Naomi,' Sev said, and Naomi closed her eyes and then opened them but she still felt giddy.

Breathless and dizzy just at the sound of his deep voice.

'Do we have a deal?' Sev asked.

She was playing with fire, Naomi knew, but then again

it was an internal one, and she doubted whether a man as suave as Sevastyan was, at this moment, self-combusting at the thought of her.

It was just a matter of keeping her private feelings in check and, Naomi knew, she was extremely good at that.

She'd been doing that for most of her twenty-five years after all.

She thought of telling her father that she'd scored such a prestigious job, that maybe, finally, she might see a flare of approval in his eyes.

It might be the new start they needed.

'Naomi,' Sev pushed. 'Do we have a deal or not?'

'We do,' Naomi croaked. 'When would I start?'

She hoped that he'd say a month, or even in two weeks' time.

Or Monday.

She just wanted a little space to clear her head before she faced him again but then came the deep of his voice.

'Turn around and get back in the elevator,' Sev replied, and then, like some expert quizmaster, he hit the stopwatch on her life. 'Your time with me starts now.'

CHAPTER ONE

NAOMI WOKE UP lying in a very warm, comfortable bed. She just stared out into the darkness and waited for dawn with butterflies dancing in her chest.

Last night she had called Andrew and had told him that they were over.

As expected, he hadn't taken it well at all.

But, then, he hadn't taken her coming to New York to spend time with her father well either. In fact, they had broken up the night before Naomi had flown out. The next morning he had turned up at Heathrow with an engagement ring, telling her that he would wait.

Now she didn't look back at that time with tenderness. She had been sideswiped, Naomi knew. It had taken these months apart to see that she had said yes under pressure and that she didn't need him to magnanimously grant her a year's leave of absence.

It was done and while she should feel relief and did, Naomi wasn't thinking about Andrew any more.

Instead the butterflies had turned into a flock of sparrows and she felt sick with dread at another difficult conversation she would be having at some point today.

With Sev.

Of course, Andrew had asked her if there was someone else and Naomi had hesitated for a beat too long before answering him.

No, there was no one else, she had told him, and that was the truth.

Sort of.

Naomi had been working for Sev for three months now and, yes, he'd tried it on a couple of times.

Once when they had been stuck in his jet for hours on a runway in Mali and he'd put down the book he always read on take-off and had suggested she might want to go for a lie-down.

With him on top.

Or she could be on top.

He was generous like that, he'd told her.

Another time had been in Helsinki when he'd come to her hotel suite to bring her up to date on a business meeting and to tell her that he'd changed his security code. Naomi had been making notes when Sev had declared himself permanently cured of his yen for blondes.

And had suggested bed.

Of course Naomi told him that, as flattered as she was by his offer, not only was she engaged, she would never get involved with her boss.

He was the least romantic person she had ever met.

And Naomi was completely in lust with him.

For all she had been told how cold he was, Sev didn't seem that around her.

Despite dumping Andrew, Naomi looked down at the ring on her finger and was grateful for the decision she had made last night to keep wearing it while she worked out her notice with Sev.

So, while technically there was no one else, Naomi would take all the help she could not to succumb to Sev's charms.

Oh, she'd love to sleep with Sev just to have slept with him.

It was the aftermath she did not need.

Or the absolute lack of aftermath on Sev's part.

Her phone buzzed an alarm and Naomi turned it off and then pulled back the covers and padded out to the kitchen and fixed herself a coffee.

It was a beautiful apartment, with thirteen-foot-high ceilings, mahogany doors and gorgeous fireplaces. Not that she used them. Instead she relied on the regular heating, worried that she'd burn the whole complex down.

Sev had the penthouse suite and he had been right— apart from the occasions when they prearranged to meet in the foyer their paths rarely crossed out of work.

The problem *was* work and very long days spent together and even longer trips abroad.

Or rather Naomi's problem was her feelings for him.

She took her drink back to bed and wondered if she was about to make the biggest mistake of her life by quitting her job, and then, as if in answer, her phone rang.

It was 6:00 a.m. on a Monday morning, but that meant nothing to Sev.

Naomi was available pretty much 24/7 and there was no space from him. There was little to no time to catch her breath from the roller-coaster ride, no time to slow her racing heart down and regroup.

'Hi, Sev.'

'What time is it?' Sev asked.

Naomi bit back a smart retort—oh, she could have said that she wasn't his personal talking clock but she conceded that he paid her enough for her to be one, if he so chose. 'It's six,' Naomi said. 'Six a.m.,' she added.

Just in case.

'Okay, can you cancel my morning?' Sev said. 'Actually, just cancel the rest of my day. I'll be back on board tomorrow.'

Oh, no!

Now she understood the odd question about the time. He wasn't even in the same time zone.

'Sev, where are you?'

'On my way back.'

'But from where? You're supposed to be meeting Sheikh Allem at eleven and then we're having dinner tonight with him and his wife. It's been booked in for ages, it's taken weeks to arrange.'

'I know all that.'

'So you have to be here.'

'What's the flying time from Rome to New York?' Sev asked.

Forget the time zone, Naomi thought. He wasn't even on the same continent. 'Just over eight hours,' Naomi sighed.

'So you see it's not possible.'

She could almost envisage him shrugging.

'Sev,' Naomi appealed. 'Allem rang last night to say how much he and his wife are looking forward to this visit. He's been so patient.'

Sheikh Allem had been. He had asked Sev to come to Dubai to review his hotel's security system yet Sev had been putting the visit off. Now he had flown with his wife to visit him.

They were friends more than business associates but Sev didn't need friends—he wanted Allem and his wife to back off.

They refused to get the message.

'Okay, okay,' Sev snapped. 'I'm on my way to the airport. When I get to the plane I'll ask the pilot to put his foot down or whatever it is they do. Look, I haven't a hope of getting there before three.'

'What should I say to him?'

'That's what I pay you to sort out,' Sev said. 'Just use your charm, Naomi.'

'It's all used up.'

'I have noticed,' Sev responded. 'You've been very...'

'Testy?' Naomi offered.

'I don't know what that word means.'

'Bad-tempered, irritable.'

'Yes, you have been very testy of late.'

'Because my boss keeps disappearing on me. Just what exactly are you doing in Rome?' Hell, she ran his diary, booked his flights, arranged his schedule and, Naomi knew damn well that he wasn't supposed to be there.

'You want to know *exactly*?' Sev checked.

Naomi closed her eyes. She knew, of course, that it would be about a woman.

And that was why she was being so testy. Naomi, more than anything, loathed confrontation, or rather she could not stand to be the one who brought things to the boil. In fact, she actually wanted Sev to fire her. It would be better than having to resign later today.

'I mean, why are you in Rome?' Naomi said. 'I'm just trying to work out what to tell Sheikh Allem.'

'Well, I guess it just seemed a good idea at the time.'

'And I guess that time was Saturday night.'

'You know me so well. I was at a party and—'

'I've changed my mind,' Naomi snapped. 'I don't need to know. I'll come up with something for Allem.'

'You're sounding very English,' Sev said. 'Work something out. Oh, and can you organise some flowers from me?'

Naomi closed her eyes.

'If you can send two dozen white roses...'

He really didn't need to tell her that—it was always the same routine with Sev.

On a Monday Naomi would arrange flowers for whoever he had seen over the weekend. Around Wednesday he might ask her to organise a hotel for the following one.

The next Monday it might be a case of more flowers but generally he'd lost interest by then.

'What's her name?' Naomi asked, as she reached for her pen. 'And what message do you want?'

'Actually,' Sev said, 'don't worry about the flowers. Apart from Allem, am I missing out on anything else?'

'Just a scheduled beginning-of-the-month meeting with me.' She had been going to tell him then that she was resigning.

Sev was silent.

'It's November,' Naomi said.

'I know that.'

'I'm just checking that you do.'

'Anything else?'

'No, everything was cleared for Allem.'

'I'll be there as soon as I can. Tell Allem...' He thought for a moment. 'Just tell him what you have to and if he acts up remind him he's the one who wants to see me.'

He didn't say goodbye, he simply rang off, and, no, Naomi thought, she wouldn't miss this part of the job—reorganising his schedule at a moment's notice and letting people down. At least that was how it felt to her. His clients didn't seem to mind in the least. That he was unattainable made him all the more desirable. The more elusive he was the more in demand he became.

'Bloody Sev,' Naomi grumbled, then sank back on her pillows to enjoy a rare lie-in.

There was no need to rush in now. She could work

here for a couple of hours, so she lay back and waited for sunrise and thought about what she was about to do.

Most would say she was mad to give up such an amazing job and all the perks that came with it.

For the past three months Naomi had been telling herself the same.

Yet she was fast learning that location, location didn't equate to happiness. A designer wardrobe and manicured nails and a fabulous haircut didn't magically put the world to rights.

On sight she had fallen for Sev.

Hard.

And, like her many predecessors, Naomi knew how futile hoping for anything other than the briefest of flings with him would be.

She should get out before she succumbed, Naomi had decided. She was already conflicted enough, trying to forge some sort of relationship with her father as well as ending things with Andrew.

A temporary fling with Sev she certainly didn't need, for though it might be temporary for him, an encounter of the sexual kind, Naomi knew, would add a permanent tattoo to her heart.

He wasn't cold at all. In fact, sometimes it felt as if he had been put on this earth with the sole reason to make her smile.

Which he did.

A lot.

He was inappropriate, yes.

But he was no more inappropriate than her own thoughts.

The chair in his office still felt battery operated.

His voice made her stomach curl.

And as for emotionless…

Whether he was or he wasn't, he brought out all of her emotions effortlessly.

The morning was arriving and it looked crisp and clear from the warmth of bed. Somebody must have been out with a paintbrush last night for Central Park was a rich palette of burnt reds and oranges and she wondered what it might look like to lie in bed in winter with the bedroom fire lit, looking out at the trees stripped bare and heavy with snow.

She wasn't going to be here to find out.

And she would tell him so today.

CHAPTER TWO

THE VIEW WAS just as impressive on Sev's part of the planet.

Not that he saw much of it.

He wore dark glasses and the tinted windows of the hotel's black Mercedes blocked out the midday sun as he called Naomi while being driven to his plane.

Sev looked out briefly at the sights of Rome as he was driven through the busy streets. He'd possibly get there quicker if he jumped on a moped but, though cross with himself for sleeping in and thus being so late for Allem, he wasn't about to go to such extremes.

Instead he had pulled out his phone and decided that Naomi would just have to fix things.

She wasn't best pleased with him but a moody PA he did not need so he snapped off the phone, relieved as his car pulled onto the tarmac near his waiting plane. What the hell had possessed him to call out his crew on a Saturday night to fly here when now he couldn't even remember her name?

It wasn't as if it was for sex that he'd gone to such extremes. Sex had been taken care of long before they'd boarded.

And it hadn't been about conversation—he wasn't particularly fluent in Italian.

Sev wasn't feeling very good about another reckless night and he certainly didn't need Reverend Sister Naomi's silent tsk tsk of disapproval.

Shannon, his flight attendant, greeted him and knew him well enough to wait and ask how he wanted his coffee before making it.

It varied.

'Long and black,' Sev said, taking off his jacket. 'With one sugar.' He took a seat but by the time he had Sev had already changed his mind and called Shannon back.

'A strong latte, two sugars.'

Maybe the milk would help his stomach but Sev knew he was, thanks to Naomi, suffering from a rare spasm of guilt.

He liked Allem and his wife and knew that they were in New York primarily to catch up with him as, thanks to the excuse of work commitments, Sev had declined their last two invitations to visit them in Dubai.

It had been Allem who had given him his first break.

Sev's past should mean he lived on the streets but he never had.

His grades at school had been outstanding and had meant he had received a scholarship to a very good school and then an internship.

It had been cell phones that Sev had been into then and he had come up with the design that Allem had run with.

Yes, Sev's cynical voice reminded him, that design had meant that Allem had made an absolute fortune out of his idea.

Yet Allem had then bankrolled Sev, allowing him to delve deeply into the cyber world. Now his genius sat in a range of one step behind or two steps ahead of the bad boys. This meant his services were in expensive demand from governments to law enforcement, airlines, royalty and show business. Sev fought his virtual enemies with talent and respect.

It was an endless, relentless game and one, more often than not, he won.

His success wasn't down to Allem—he owed him nothing, Sev thought, draining his coffee, as Jason, the captain, spoke and told him he was hoping to catch a tail wind and they should arrive just before three.

Shannon came to take his cup and any moment now they'd be on their way.

'Do you want me to fix lunch after take-off?' she offered, but Sev shook his head.

'I don't want anything to eat, I'm just going to go to bed. Don't wake me unless the plane is going down,' Sev said. 'Actually, don't wake me even if it is.'

He opened up his book, the one he always read during take-off, but not even that could distract him today.

Sev avoided friendships, he avoided getting close to anyone, yet Allem insisted on sticking around.

As soon as he was able to he made his way to the bedroom.

He stripped, had a quick shower and then got into bed but sleep eluded him.

That needle of guilt was still there so he called Naomi again.

'I can't sleep,' Sev admitted.

'Where are you now?'

'An hour out of Rome. Have you spoken to Allem?'

'Not yet. I've sent an email telling him that you've been delayed,' Naomi said. 'I'll call him closer to nine when I've worked out a reason why.'

There was a slightly tart edge to her voice.

'Go into my bureau,' Sev said. He had actually bought a gift for Jamal and Allem. 'There should be a polished box there you could wrap for me. You could give it to him as a little sweetener until I arrive.'

'Okay.'

'Is it there?' Sev asked, wondering if he might have left it in his apartment.

'I'll look when I get to the office.'

'You're not in yet?'

'No,' Naomi said. 'Caught.'

'Caught what?'

'Having a lie-in.' Naomi said, but then hurriedly added, 'I'm up now, though.'

'Liar.'

'You trained me well,' Naomi responded. They were both in bed and both knew it.

'Go up to my apartment before you head into work. It might be in my desk there. If not, then it's in the bureau at work. It's got a statue in it.'

'Okay. So what lie do you want me to feed Allem?'

But Sev's mind was on other things.

Yes, he'd been feeling bad about Allem but knowing that Naomi was in bed, hopefully as naked as he, was, well, a bit of a turn-on.

She drove him crazy.

He could not read her.

It was like a weather report telling you it was sultry and hot and then stepping out to sleet and ice.

'Can I ask you something?'

'No,' Naomi answered. 'About Allem. What am I to tell him?'

Oh, that was right. The reason for his call.

'Just tell him there was a family emergency that I had to attend to. He's big on family. Tell him that my mother was taken ill and I'm on my way back from Russia.'

'Sev, is your mother alive?'

'Yes?'

'Is she sick?'

'She could be.'

He heard a slight noise as she sucked in her breath. 'You don't like the idea.'

'It's not for me to judge…'

'Oh, but, baby, you do,' Sev snapped. 'Over and over you do. And do you know what? I don't need it. I'm warning you—'

'Officially?' Naomi checked, more than happy for him to fire her now, even the dark rise of his voice turned her on.

'Unofficially,' Sev said.

God, but he even liked rowing with her.

Sev didn't row. Usually he simply couldn't be bothered to.

They both lay in tense angry silence but neither ended the call and then Sev said it again but his voice wasn't angry now.

'Can I ask you something?' No, he wasn't angry. His voice had that low edge to it that had her pull up her knees.

'Go ahead.' Naomi sighed.

'It's personal.'

She had guessed that it might be.

'I'm just curious about something.'

Somehow he didn't offend her.

Naomi was curious about him too.

She just lay there naked in bed, trying to imagine how that low voice might sound while making love to her, and she was terribly, terribly tempted to find out.

To just finally give in to the suggestive air they created.

'Ask away.'

'Well, I'm assuming, if you're engaged, that you must love your fiancé.'

She didn't answer.

'And fancy him.'

Naomi said nothing.

'So how do you...?'

'How do I what, Sev?'

'You've been in New York for three months and in that time I can't recall him coming over to see you.'

'He hasn't.'

'So,' Sev asked, 'how do you manage?'

Manage!

Oh, it was as basic as that to Sev, Naomi thought. An itch to be scratched, a line on his to-do list to be regularly ticked off.

'Sev,' Naomi crisply replied, when she would far rather dive under the covers and prolong the call, 'I'm giving *you* an official warning now.'

She hung up on him. Sev tossed the phone down in frustration.

Bloody Naomi, Sev thought as he lay there. He was hard for her and had been left hanging. And then he remembered why he'd come to Rome.

She had been brunette.

It was as simple and as messed up as that.

He was over Naomi and her moods.

Sev didn't need some sanctimonious PA sitting on her moral throne. She was there to run his life, not have him account for it.

Who cared what she thought?

He cared about no one.

Only that wasn't quite right.

God, but he hated this month already.

Sev *hated* November.

He always had and he always would.

In Russia it was Mother's Day at the end of November.

At school, the 'home kids', as he and his friends had called the students who'd had families, would sit and make cards for their mothers as the *'detsky dom'* kids stuck rice onto paper for, well, no one in particular.

There had been four at his table, they had been together since nursery school.

Sevastyan had always been the nerdy one, Nikolai had liked ships and then there had been the twins, Roman and Daniil, who were going to be famous boxers one day.

Some day.

Never.

'If you don't have a mother then make a card for someone you care about,' the teacher had suggested each year.

The *'detsky dom'* kids' cards had never got made.

A few years back Sevastyan had found out that he did have a mother, but he now knew that she wouldn't have appreciated a card with stuck-on rice anyway.

He'd send flowers, of course, but rather than rely on Naomi he would try to work out himself what to put in the note.

Each year it became harder to work out what to write.

Thanks for being there?

She hadn't been.

With love to you on this special day?

It wasn't a special day to her.

And there was no love.

November also meant that it was his niece's birthday.

Her eighteenth! Sev suddenly remembered.

He'd stop at Tiffany on the way to the office Sev thought, then decided not to bother.

Whatever he sent would just end up being pawned or put up on some auction site.

Yes, for so many reasons he hated November.

Sev closed his eyes but he still could not sleep.

He stared into the dark and could remember as if it were yesterday, rather than half a lifetime ago, hearing his friend quietly crying in the night.

These had been boys who had stopped crying from the cradle and so Sev had not known whether his friend would appreciate that he knew that he was.

'What's wrong?' Sev had asked. 'Nikolai, what has happened?'

'Nothing.'

'It doesn't sound like nothing.'

'Leave it.'

He had.

To Sev's utter, utter regret, he had.

In the morning Nikolai had been gone.

A week later his body had washed up and Sergio had come back with his bag, in it a ship Nikolai had been making out of matches.

Sev lay there and thought of his friend and his sad end.

And the thought of the others he still missed to this day.

On the twelfth of November, the day Nikolai had run away, Sev would be in London for yet another futile attempt to meet with his past.

He might give it a miss, Sev thought, but he was as superstitious as he was Russian.

If he didn't go, of course it would be the one year that Daniil showed up.

CHAPTER THREE

SHEIKH ALLEM WAS extremely gracious about the change in plans.

In fact, when Naomi had called him at nine he hadn't seemed in the least surprised. He'd told Naomi that he would come to the office at four but in the meantime, would she mind taking Jamal shopping?

'Of course.'

Naomi had dressed in a navy shift dress and flat ballet pumps and she headed up to Sev's apartment to check if the gift he had bought for Allem was there.

His apartment took up the entire floor.

She was often in there, packing his case, doing little jobs, showing through a designer because he'd decided he had changed his mind about a wall or a light or whatever it was that he might suddenly decide that he wanted changed. She basically took care of many details of Sev's life so that he didn't have to.

His maid was in there, changing the flowers and making sure everything was perfect for his return.

Naomi said hi and went through to Sev's study.

There was no polished wooden box that she could see in any of the drawers.

She looked on top of the desk.

There was no box there either, just a rather scruffy little ship.

It was odd, Naomi thought, picking it up and examining it. It was old and poorly put together, unlike anything else in the apartment.

She put it down again and then headed into his bedroom, deciding to take the opportunity to take a couple of fresh shirts to the office.

His bedroom was her favourite room.

Not because of him.

Well, maybe.

But it kind of fascinated Naomi.

The mahogany door she opened didn't close as the same thing.

Bored with the trimmings, he had made a few alterations to a heritage building and the other side of the door was ebony.

As were the rest of the trimmings.

Another maid was in there, changing the bedding on his big black wooden bed.

It was beautiful.

The view was amazing and the curtains were black on ivory with a dash of pistachio-green—the only dart of colour in the entire room, apart from the view.

Because it was the beginning of the month, Naomi took out her tablet and made a quick inventory.

He had one woman who shopped for his clothing, who Naomi liaised with. He had another who dealt with food and beverages.

His PA dealt with personal items.

She went to his dressing table and saw the cologne she had ordered last month from Paris. The container was still half-full but she made a note and then, joy, went to his bedside table and made another note of items that needed to be replenished!

She would not miss this part of her job in the least. In fact, she was so annoyed that she forgot to go through to the bathroom and instead took the shirts and headed into work.

Sure enough, in the bureau in his office was a gleaming wooden box and Naomi had a peek inside and frowned.

He'd bought it in Mali, she remembered.

And she'd wondered why at the time.

It was a fertility statue.

Naomi considered whether she should call Sev and tell him that this might not be the best gift to give the sheikh but what the hell, it was his faux pas and she was still cross with him and not in the mood for another little chat with a naked Sev.

Naomi wrapped the gift and decided that Sev could give it to him and deal with the consequences and she placed it back in the bureau. She then went to meet Jamal and spent a few hours shopping and chatting before Naomi saw her back to her hotel. She got a call from Sev's driver to say that his plane had landed but she came back to an office still devoid of Sev.

Damn.

Allem would be here soon.

She felt terrible, lying for Sev. Till today she hadn't even known that Sev had a mother. She knew everything and nothing about him.

He never spoke about family.

She was never asked to send presents or flowers for anyone other than girlfriends.

Naomi pulled up his account at the florist and looked at May.

No, judging by the messages sent that month, a Mother's Day bouquet hadn't been sent.

It was none of her business, Naomi told herself.

She just wanted to know some more.

She was alerted that Allem had arrived and Naomi greeted him. He was robed and wearing a *kafeya* and just so polished and well mannered she wondered if he was royal.

'His plane has just landed,' Naomi said, and fired Sev a text as they waited.

And waited.

Allem didn't seem to mind in the least.

'How long have you been working for Sevastyan?' Allem asked, as Naomi poured tea.

'Three months.'

And with her notice served it would be three months and two weeks. Naomi had absolutely decided that she was going to do it.

Finally Sev appeared, as rumpled as if he had flown economy to get here rather than on his luxury private jet.

Still beautiful, Naomi thought, but though she smiled a greeting it didn't quite meet her eyes.

His neck was a mess from his weekend of passion and she knew now why it had taken so long for him to get from the airport—from the bag he was carrying it was clear that he had stopped off at Tiffany.

Not for a second did she presume he'd stopped to buy something for her.

'I'm very sorry to hear about your mother,' Allem offered. 'How is she?'

'Touch and go,' Sev replied, and jiggled his hand. No, he didn't say sorry for being seven hours late. 'Let's go through to my office.' He led Allem through and as he closed the door he gave Naomi a smile of thanks.

No doubt he thought he had got away with it and Allem believed that his mother was sick—didn't he get it that Allem was just too polite to mention the bite marks on his neck?

Naomi was completely over this job.

No, she wasn't burnt out.

It was far more than that.

He'd lie about his own mother.

Sev was a bastard.

Felicity had told her that at her first interview.

Even Sev had warned her that he was on her very first day.

'I prefer computers,' he'd yawned, as he'd called on her, on her very first day, to handle a teary previous date who'd kept calling him on the office phone. 'No tears, no dramas.' He'd seen her cheeks redden. 'I'm not talking about porn.'

'I never said that you were.'

'I'm just saying that I prefer computers to people.'

Naomi thought back to her first day and now and the months in between and, really, even if she knew so many details about his life, she knew him no better at all. She didn't even know how he took his coffee.

It, like Sev, changed on a whim.

Sev closed the door on Naomi's silent disapproval and as Allem took a seat Sev opened up the bureau to see that Naomi had wrapped the gift for him.

'I got this for Jamal when I was in Mali,' Sev said and handed over the gift and watched as Allem opened it. 'I remember you saying that she likes statues and I...' his voice trailed off as Allem started laughing when he took out the ebony statue that had caught Sev's restless eye a few weeks ago. 'What's so funny?'

'Sevastyan, this is a most inappropriate gift to give to my wife,' Allem said, but with a smile. 'It's a fertility statue.'

'Really! Well, I want it out of this office, then.'

'Actually, Jamal will laugh when I tell her that you bought this with her in mind. You are in fact a little too late. I'm delighted to tell you that we are expecting a baby in March.'

Sev said all the right things.

Well, he tried.

Allem had been wild once, Sev thought.

Perhaps that was why they *had* got on so well.

They had used to hit the clubs wherever in the world they were.

But in the past couple of years it had been lengthy dinners with Allem and Jamal and whatever date Sev brought along.

Now, Allem spoke about morning sickness and how Jamal had lost weight and was a touch teary and Sev had to stop his eyes from crossing as Allem droned on.

'Though Jamal enjoyed shopping with Naomi and is very much looking forward to dinner tonight.'

Sev smothered a yawn.

'Will Naomi be joining us tonight?' Allem checked.

'Of course,' Sev answered. He knew better than to expect Jamal to come out for dinner without female company.

'So you and Naomi are dating?' Allem pushed the conversation to the personal when Sev would far rather that they spoke about work. 'I see she is wearing an engagement ring.'

'Well, it's not mine,' Sev snapped. 'What on earth gave you that idea?'

'It's just that you don't often bring your PA to our dinners.'

That was true, Sev thought. Generally he rustled up a date, promising her that if she would sit through the very tame dinner, he would make it up to her later that night.

It had been easier, though, to take Naomi lately.

She really was exceptionally good with his clients.

For all her faults, for all her little digs about his life-style, Naomi certainly knew how to smooth the feathers that he tended to ruffle along his decadent way.

Finally they got around to work and, yes, Sev agreed, he would need to come to Dubai. 'I really am booked out, though, Allem,' he explained. 'I need four clear days at least and I don't have anything like that until March.'

'Which is when the baby is due,' Allem said. 'Sev, I know you are busy but I have been asking for a while now.'

Sev nodded and pulled up his diary onto his computer screen.

This week he had to go to Washington DC and there could be no getting out of that. Next week he was heading off to London, which, despite earlier thoughts about not going, really was non-negotiable to him. But maybe he was growing a conscience—Allem had been asking him to come to Dubai as his guest for months, as well as do some work for him.

And he had been inexcusably late today.

'I'll get Naomi to reschedule some of my clients,' Sev offered. 'We can be there on Saturday.'

'Excellent.'

Naomi looked up when the two men came out of Sev's office. Allem was all smiles.

He came and thanked her for the tea she had made and for taking care of Jamal.

'We're looking forward to dinner,' Allem said.

'So am I.' Naomi smiled.

Instead of only seeing Allem as far as the elevator, which was as far as Sev usually went when saying farewell to clients, he was clearly going to see Allem to his car.

Were they friends? Naomi pondered.

They seemed such an unlikely mix.

'I shan't be long,' Sev said to Naomi on his way out, and, behind Allem's robed back, he made a gesture with his hand that was Sev language for *Pour me a cognac.*

Naomi went in to his office and poured him a drink but then, unable to help herself, she slid open the drawer and took out the bag. She looked at the pretty robin-egg-blue box wrapped in a white bow and tortured herself with images of engagement rings.

Was that why he'd flown to Rome?

Oh, God, the white roses were bad enough but she could not stand the thought of Sev actually getting serious about someone.

He had never bought anyone jewellery in all her time here; it had been white roses and that was all.

'Snooping?' Sev asked as he came, unheard by Naomi, into the office, and she was just too tired of it all to jump or even blush.

'I wasn't sure if you wanted me to wrap it.'

'You think you'd do a better job than Tiffany's?' Sev teased.

As she went to put the box back in the bag Sev held out his hand and she handed it to him.

'I think I've changed my mind about them.'

He tore off the bow, opened the box and stared for a moment then handed it to Naomi for her thoughts.

She'd rather not share them.

Silently she stared at the earrings—two heart-shaped, pink-diamond-encrusted studs.

They were gorgeous.

Seriously so.

'They're beautiful,' Naomi said, but Sev wasn't sure and he took back the box and looked at them again.

'I think that they're a bit too pink, but then again she's young and the guy who served me said that was what they all wanted at the moment.'

So, no white roses for Miss Roma, Naomi thought.

'You don't look very convinced,' Sev said, noting Naomi's lack of enthusiasm.

Just how hard did she have to act?

'Sev, they're stunning.' Naomi spoke, she hoped, with conviction. 'Any woman would be thrilled to have them.'

Especially from you.

She looked at the little frown line between his eyes as still he examined the earrings. This man who cared so little for other's feelings really did seem to care about this gift and its reception, Naomi could tell.

And so it really was time to leave.

'Okay, let's run through my schedule,' Sev said, snapping closed the box and leaving it for Naomi to re-tie the bow. 'It's changed. We're going to be flying to Dubai on Saturday and then from there straight on to London. I have to be there for the twelfth.'

'In the morning?' Naomi checked.

'No, no,' Sev said. 'I want to get there on the eleventh, just to allow for delays and things.'

Naomi raised her eyebrows—Sev was usually the delay.

'I know that you'll have to rearrange a few things but I can't not go to Washington and I really can't keep putting Allem off.'

'I get that,' Naomi agreed. 'Did he like the statue?'

'He loved it,' Sev answered, which only confused her more.

'Sev, could I have word with you?'

'Can it wait?' Sev asked. 'We've got to meet Allem in less than an hour.'

'No.' Naomi shook her head. 'It can't wait.'

If she didn't do it now then it would just get harder and, given they were going to be in Dubai, if there was going to be even a hope of finding her replacement she needed to get things under way soon.

'You'll have to watch me get changed, then,' Sev said, picking up the drink she had poured and taking a long sip as he started to undo his tie.

'Hardly a first.' She didn't take a seat, she was too nervous to, and so instead Naomi stood and leant on his desk.

Tie off, he pulled open a door to a dressing room and selected a fresh shirt with no thought as to how it had got there.

It wasn't his problem.

Sev peered into the mirror.

'I'd better shave.'

Naomi said nothing as he stripped off his shirt and dropped it to the floor and then walked over towards her to top up his drink.

He just walked towards her with no thought about the effect a half-naked Sev had on her.

That wasn't his problem either.

His skin was pale and on anyone else it might be too pale yet on Sev all it did was enhance his lithe, toned body and shadowed his chest to perfection. His arms were as long as his legs and his nipples were the same deep merlot of his mouth and just as tempting. His trou-

sers sat a little too low on his hips, just that fraction between notches on a belt, and those were the details she
fought not to notice as his hand reached for a heavy glass
and held it up to her.

'Have one,' Sev said. 'It's going to be a very long,
dry night.'

Sometimes they had a drink about now, especially if
they were going out for dinner, but Naomi declined with
a small shake of her head. Even if a cognac to settle her
nerves might be nice, she'd rather hold onto her inhibi-
tions than lose them around him.

This was going to be harder than she'd allowed for.

She loved her job.

Her career.

It just wasn't working.

Oh, there was a reason she could not abide certain
parts of her job. Had it been Edward, her previous boss,
or any of her bosses before Sev, this would be an unnoted
part of a long day—brief downtime before she headed
out for a dinner with his clients.

Instead she was trying to work out where to place her
eyes when they wanted to rest on him.

'If it's about this morning,' Sev said, lathering up his
chin, 'there's no need. You don't have to apologise.'

Her lips moved into an unseen but incredulous smile.

'We're reducing your use of the "sorry" word, remember?'

He really took the cake at times!

Yes, she could tell him he had been the inappropriate one this morning yet she was looking at his back and
fighting not to go over there.

Naomi was truly tired of fighting her feelings.

Feelings, Naomi knew, that could get seriously hurt.

And neither did those feelings allow her to do her job

properly. Naomi knew she had been surly this morning about his late arrival when, as his PA, she had no right to be.

'That's not what I'm here about, Sev.' Naomi cleared her throat and watched as Sev picked up the razor. 'I'm handing in my notice.'

She watched as the razor hesitated over his jaw but then he commenced shaving as she carried on with her little prepared speech.

'You said at the start that you'd be surprised if I lasted more than three months.' Naomi reminded him.

'I did.'

'And I've loved the work, I really have, it's just…'

He turned from the mirror. 'Naomi, you don't need to give a reason to leave.'

He could be so kind at times—awkward, embarrassing things like resigning he dealt with so well.

'Will you be sticking around to find a replacement?' Sev asked, as he carried on with his shave.

'I'll do what I can this week but if we're going to Dubai, it might be pushing it, unless you don't need me to go.'

'No, no,' Sev said. 'I need you to be there. I go to Washington the day after tomorrow…' He thought for a moment. 'I'll come back on Thursday night. If you can have at least two applicants lined up by then, that would be good.'

'Sure.'

She'd have little trouble. Applications to work for Sevastyan Derzhavin arrived in her inbox all the time. 'I'll go from Dubai to London and there we can part ways.'

'You're coming back to New York, though?' Sev checked.

'Oh, yes.' Naomi nodded. 'I want to have Christmas with my family here.'

'How's that all going?' Sev asked, turning back to the mirror and getting on with shaving.

'Good! I'm going there tomorrow night.'

'For dinner?'

'I'm babysitting,' Naomi answered. 'They're going to the theatre.'

Sev said nothing. He loathed how she jumped to her father's every wish. They could be in the middle of a meeting and if her father texted or called, even if she tried not to respond, Sev could feel the tension in her.

Then he chose not to say nothing. 'You like the theatre,' he pointed out.

'Not really.'

'It says that you do on your résumé.'

'And I told you that I lied about that.'

'Aren't you going to ask about a reference?'

Naomi nodded.

'I'll do that first thing tomorrow,' Sev promised.

He rinsed his face and then dried it, splashed on a load of cologne, took a sip of his drink and then put on his fresh shirt.

And that was that.

She'd resigned. It was done with.

And he'd barely so much as blinked.

CHAPTER FOUR

'ARE YOU GOING to get changed?' Sevastyan asked.

Naomi nodded.

His complete lack of reaction only confirmed that she was right to leave.

It was easy come, easy go to Sev, and that hurt a lot.

As she headed out of his office to get changed for their night out, only then did she remember. 'I haven't got my dress here,' Naomi said. 'I was supposed to pick it up from the cleaner's in my lunch break but I went shopping with Jamal and I forgot.'

'No problem.' He dealt with it as easily as the news that she had resigned. 'Do you have something at home ready to put on? We can stop on the way to the restaurant.'

Of course she had something at home—given her lavish clothing allowance—and they headed to her apartment. She rather wished he hadn't shaved or smelled so divine as they took the elevator to the tenth floor, where Naomi lived, rather than his penthouse.

'So?' Sevastyan asked on the way up. 'Where are we eating tonight?'

Naomi told him the name of a very upmarket Middle Eastern restaurant.

'That's not very imaginative.' Sev pulled a face. 'Won't they be sick of Middle Eastern food?'

'I doubt people get sick of their home cuisine,' Naomi said as she let them into her apartment. 'I had actually booked a French restaurant but Jamal is feeling a bit…' She chose not to tell Sev the news that Jamal had shared with her as they'd shopped. He was insensitive at the best of times and completely devoid of social niceties at his worst. 'She just wanted a menu she knows.'

'Fair enough.'

'Help yourself to a drink,' Naomi said. 'I'll just go and get changed.'

Sevastyan would have helped himself to a drink had there actually been anything decent to choose from. He opened her fridge and there wasn't even a bottle of wine in there.

He walked back out to the lounge room and saw the picture of a man presumably her fiancé, lying on the table by the phone.

How sweet, he thought with a brittle edge. She must look at him as she spoke to him on the phone.

Then Sev remembered he and Naomi's little near miss this morning and, though his question had been inappropriate, it had been a genuine one. Not just the sex. He knew he would never be close enough to anyone to get engaged but this jerk in the photo was.

It had been Naomi's birthday in October.

Sev hadn't known, he'd just known something was up, and when he'd pushed her, Naomi had told him she was upset that neither of her parents had called to wish her a happy birthday.

'I'm sure something nice will happen,' Sev had said. He had been sure.

Surely her fiancé was on a plane right now, about to whisk her off for one night.

And he wasn't thinking as a snob with a private jet.

Naomi had told him herself that her fiancé, Andrew, had an important job, so presumably it paid enough for a flight on your future wife's birthday.

Apparently not.

Sev had taken her to the theatre, which he loathed, and then dinner, which he'd enjoyed.

And then back to the same building, different floors by midnight.

Which had confused him.

He and Naomi…

It was something that needed addressing.

He was about to stick his middle finger up at the image of Andrew, but changed it to look as if he was scratching his ear as Naomi came out.

She was wearing a very elegant, fitted dark grey dress. However, she needed help with the zip and was carrying her shoes and a necklace as she attempted to get ready in two minutes flat.

'Do we have time for me to do my hair?' Naomi asked, slipping her shoes on.

'No.' He looked over to where she was struggling with the zip.

'Come here,' he offered.

She would really rather not but, choosing not to make a fuss, she went over and held up her hair. Sev went to the zip, but instead of pulling it the rest of the way up, he pulled it the rest of the way down. 'Whoops.'

'Sev!' Naomi sighed. They really didn't have time for his games.

But Sev was in no rush now that he was looking at her delicate pink neck; her hand was shaking a touch as she held up her hair and, no, he decided, he hadn't misread the sensual air he had sniffed back in the office. Naomi Johnson was as turned on as he—which was very.

Her back was bare, apart from the strap of her bra, and he was very tempted to undo that too.

She had a lovely back, Sev thought. Not that backs were generally his thing. He rather wanted to turn her around but instead he ran a light finger along her spine.

Naomi closed her eyes to the bliss.

'Hey, Naomi,' Sev said. His voice was a bit lower than usual and there was definite tension in the air. 'You do realise that now you've resigned, we can spend the next two weeks in bedded bliss.'

'I missed that when I went through my contract,' Naomi replied. 'Just how did you come to that conclusion exactly?'

'Well, you told me, when we were in Helsinki, that you would never sleep with your boss.'

'Actually,' Naomi corrected him, 'that conversation happened on the runway in Mali and I believe what I said was I didn't want to get involved with you.'

'Because you're engaged?'

It would never enter his head, Naomi realised, that someone might just simply not want him.

He was probably right, she knew, for she was fighting with herself not to turn around. Oh, she had been wise to keep her engagement ring on. Not that it warded him off. He had no scruples at all. His hand was now at the base of her spine, fiddling again with the zip, but then he got bored with even pretending that he was going to do it up.

Sev had wanted Naomi for a very long time. Only now that she had told him she was leaving, he seemed to want her even more.

He was more than used to his assistants resigning.

It had never troubled him at all in the past but now it did.

He had consoled himself, however, that now she was leaving they could leave a bit of the business behind and concentrate on pleasure, but Naomi had just closed the door.

He wanted it open.

'In Helsinki I told you I'd cured myself of blondes...' His finger moved up to the nape of her neck and he toyed with a stray dark curl.

Naomi stood there as he blew on her neck, or was that just his breath?

'I thought we had to be at the restaurant,' Naomi said. 'You said I didn't even have time to do my hair...'

'I'm not thinking about your hair now.'

Neither was she.

She was so tired of fighting it.

Maybe she would order her own roses once it was over, Naomi thought.

And it would be over.

Being crazy about Sevastyan was a terminal disease with no cure. She might just opt for some temporary pain relief, though.

He moved in closer behind her but not too fast. Sev didn't want her to startle to his hard-on and change her mind, but he could feel the shift in her.

'You've lost weight,' he observed, stroking the curve of her waist and moving a little higher.

'I know,' Naomi said, wondering how just the warmth of his hand on her skin could turn her on so. His hand had moved to the front of her body. Higher than her waist but lower than where she now wanted it to be. Her breasts ached, anticipating his touch. 'I thought that I'd be putting it on…' She halted her words—she was hardly going to tell Sev that with the amount of comfort eating she'd been doing lately, on top of the lavish dinners and lunches she shared with him, that should generally mean that she should be spilling out of her clothes. Instead they were hanging off her.

It was Sev who stopped the intimate moment. As his hand paused a tiny frown registered unseen on his brow. Why would Naomi think she should be putting on weight? he asked himself, and then he remembered the conversation he had just had today with Allem.

Yes, Naomi had certainly been moody of late.

Oh, God! Eternally superstitious, Sevastyan thought of the fertility statue that had been sitting in his office for weeks.

Was she pregnant?

Was that why she was leaving?

He glanced over to the picture of Andrew on the coffee table and then up went Naomi's zipper.

A pregnant PA he did not need and a pregnant lover he did not want!

'Come on,' he said in a gruff voice. 'We're already late.'

It was meant to be a very lovely dinner.

But in actual fact it was not.

It was one of those nights that you really wished you'd just stayed home.

Sev sat sulking and silent and it was Naomi who moved the conversation.

'It was cell phones then,' Allem said, turning to Sev, who was calling to the waiter for more water.

Naomi was quite sure there was a dash or three of vodka in his. He was in a horrible mood and she had no idea what had happened. One moment she'd been about to give in to three months of building desire but just as she had, Sev had changed his mind.

She would never understand him.

Thank God. Very soon, she could stop trying to.

'Remember, Sev?' Allem prompted.

'I remember coming up with the design…' Sev shrugged.

'It would have stayed a design without my money behind it,' Allem pointed out.

'True,' Sev admitted.

'So how did you get your start?' Naomi asked, when she would have liked to kick him under the table for being so distant and rude.

It was like pulling teeth sometimes to get Sev to open up.

'You got a scholarship, didn't you?' Jamal asked, and Sev nodded. He hated, more than anything, talking about his past. That was the problem with people, they always wanted to talk—he'd far prefer a night in, cracking code.

'There was an old computer in the office where I lived,' he reluctantly explained. 'When I was thirteen they were going to throw it out…'

'Office?' Naomi frowned. 'Where you lived?'

'I mean the office at the school,' Sev said, and he shot Allem a warning look.

Allem knew a little, but Sev chose not to go into his past. It was too dark, too messy, and he'd moved far, far away from all that.

'I pulled it apart and…' He shrugged, dismissing the hours and hours he had put in to rebuilding it, scouring markets and dumps, finding parts, and then, when he'd got that one running, he had moved straight to the next.

And the next.

'The scholarship helped but really…'

It had been the hours and hours spent poring over machines and books.

Any book at first.

Fairy tales, romances, biographies and crime. Whatever the staff bought in, whatever he could find, Sev had read, often again and again. Then one day he had come upon a computer programming book that had become his first bible.

His fascination remained to this day.

He didn't say all that, though, even though everyone at the table would have loved to know.

'Remember you liked that princess...' Allem grinned. 'Do you know,' he said to Naomi, 'Sevastyan hacked into the palace webpage then told them the loopholes in their system and that he could fix them.'

'I used to do that in the days when clients were thin on the ground,' Sev conceded.

'And did you get anywhere with the princess?' Naomi asked, and Sev gave her a smirk. 'Stupid question.'

She looked at him, and he looked at her.

And both were hurt, not that either would admit it.

'When you come to Dubai...' Allem said, looking from one to the other and noting again the tension. He'd seen Sev's eyes follow Naomi when she had gone to the restroom and he could hear too the little digs at each other... It was the first time he'd seen this with Sev.

Always, if Jamal had been present, Sev had had a date.

Like Sev, he could never remember their names.

He liked Naomi and he wanted to see Sev happy for once.

'This time, we want to take you out on the water, both of you...'

'I'm not coming over for a holiday,' Sev said. 'You can take Naomi.'

Naomi rolled her eyes. 'Because I do nothing all day.'

'Just take a day,' Sev said. 'Get some sun.'

He thought of her smooth, creamy back and then he looked at her pale cheeks and remembered the day they had met, how they'd burnt just as they were starting to catch fire now.

He wanted Jamal and Allem gone. He wanted to go back to where he and Naomi had left off.

Right now he wanted to put his hand beneath the table and part her thighs and the oddest thing was he thought she might let him.

Not that he would.

Hell, did pregnant women even like sex?

Sev hadn't a clue.

'We would like to see a show while we're here.' Jamal said.

'Well, you're in the right place.' Sev was still looking at Naomi. 'You love the theatre. Maybe tomorrow we could all—'

'I've already got plans.' Naomi said quickly.

'What plans?'

'I've told you, I'm babysitting for my father.'

Sev said nothing.

It was far safer not to.

He wanted to point out that she'd upended her life, moved here to spend time with her father, and apart from a couple of babysitting jobs, looking after his kids while he and his wife went out, she never saw him.

Yes, it was safer to call for the bill.

Sev's driver first took Allem and Jamal to their hotel and then it was a quiet ride back home. As they walked up the stairs towards the foyer, Sev decided that he'd had a gutful of safe.

'Can you call your father and say you can't make it tomorrow night?'

'Why would I do that?'

'Why wouldn't you?' Sev asked. 'I'll pay for a nurse or something to look after the children.'

'A nurse?' Naomi blinked. 'Sev, what planet do you come from?'

'One without babies and children. A nanny, then.'

'I want to help out.'

'Help?' Sev checked as they walked to the elevators. 'More like be trampled over.'

'They're my sisters.'

'Half-sisters,' Sev said, and they stepped into a very small space with a whole lot of tension between them. 'And that daddy-o pie of affection isn't one that's divided equally when it's the second or third time around.'

'Don't go there.' Naomi had heard enough. 'Don't try and tell me how to handle my family when you'd lie about your own mother's health.'

At the tenth floor she went to get out of the elevator but he halted her. 'Naomi, I really do need someone to come with me.'

'Then find someone, Sev,' Naomi said. 'It's close to midnight. You called me at six this morning. That's eighteen hours that I've worked today. I'm not getting this coming weekend off. Surely I can have one evening to be with my family?'

Fire me now, her eyes pleaded.

Can we just get this over with? her mind begged.

'You can have tomorrow evening off,' Sev conceded.

Sev stood there in an unmoving elevator for a moment as she walked off.

Fine.

He'd find someone.

Sev didn't have to look very far.

He pulled out his phone and by the time he'd reached the top floor he was already calling her.

'Hey, Felicity, remember Allem and Jamal?'

His ex-PA knew them well and, what the hell, she was gorgeous, blonde and, bonus points, not pregnant with someone else's child!

CHAPTER FIVE

'So, HOW ARE THINGS with Derzhavin?' her father, Anderson, asked.

It had been a very long day in the office.

Sev had been brooding and silent and Naomi was very relieved that he was going to Washington early tomorrow and that she wouldn't have to see him now until Friday.

She wasn't in the mood to chat about him but, really, Sev was the main topic of conversation between herself and her father.

Naomi sat watching as Anderson gave Amelia, her tiny, four-month-old little sister, a cuddle and kiss before handing Judy the baby to settle her for the night.

Half-sister, as Sev would say.

Oh, she never wanted to be as cynical as Sev but she also wasn't the pushover that he thought she was.

Naomi knew why she was here in New York.

She wanted to give her relationship with her father a proper chance and it hurt to watch as Judy took the baby from her father's arms only for them to be refilled instantly as three-year-old Madison clambered onto his knee for her goodnight kiss.

Naomi had been younger than Amelia when her mother had gone back to the UK, taking her with her.

She had seen her father only once since then.

When she'd been eighteen the plan had been for her to come over for a month but her father's second marriage had been on the brink of collapse. The time she had scraped and saved for had been spent in a hostel, seeing the sights, and she had met her father just for the occasional lunch.

This marriage seemed a happy one, though.

'Derzhavin,' her father prompted, and Naomi gave a little shake of her head as she dragged herself back to the conversation her father kept pursuing.

'He's as difficult as ever,' Naomi said.

'Did you give him my business card?' Anderson checked.

'He's got his own attorneys, Dad,' Naomi said. 'I'm not going to be working there for much longer—I handed my notice in yesterday.'

'You what?' Anderson frowned. 'Why on earth would you do that?'

'The hours are impossible. Some days start at six and end at midnight and that's if we're here. It's even worse when we're overseas. We go to Dubai on Saturday and then it's off to London.' Naomi shook her head. 'And that's where I get off. I'm looking for my replacement this week.'

'But it's an amazing opportunity that you're letting go.'

'I'm not here to further my career, Dad,' Naomi said.

'Are you going back to live in London?' Anderson asked, as Naomi tried to ignore the little glance that took place between him and Judy.

'No, no.' Naomi shook her head. 'I've told you—I'm here for a year. I'm looking for another job, hopefully one that has more regular hours. It might take a while but I've saved quite a bit these past three months. I might take a few weeks off.'

'But what about the apartment?' Judy checked.

'I'm looking for somewhere,' Naomi said, 'though, I have to say, it's proving harder than I thought.'

They said nothing, or rather they suddenly noticed the time and said that they had to go and then told her to help herself to nibbles and that they wouldn't be too late.

'What are you seeing?' Naomi asked.

Anderson rolled his eyes and told her the name of the musical they were going to. 'Judy loves them.'

So do I.

And she could have been there tonight with Sev, Jamal and Allem.

Naomi felt like the hired help.

Or rather the free help.

She was that awkward extended family member that everyone grimaced when her name came up or the invitations went out.

But then she thought of her three little sisters, all so blonde and gorgeous and happy to see her. Especially Kennedy, the eldest. She was very sweet and so happy to have her big sister here.

'I like it when you come and look after us,' Kennedy said as Naomi tucked her into bed.

Even that hurt.

Naomi wanted to be here, spending time with them, getting to know them, not reading a note, as she tipped the last of Kennedy's bedtime drink down the sink, asking her to remember to turn the dishwasher on.

Perhaps she was expected to wipe down the bench tops, Naomi thought. Or fold some laundry.

Instead she went and sat on the couch and looked out the window to the rushes and the water beyond.

Long Island was so beautiful and they had a huge sprawling home. Oh, Naomi could understand that maybe they hadn't wanted her here when Amelia had first came along but now…

Yes, it was too far to commute for very long. But even if they had just said that she didn't need to rush to find somewhere to live and that she could have a couple of weeks here, it would have been enough for Naomi.

She thought about Sev and their row last night. She actually wasn't angry with him for what he had said, even if it had seemed that way to him.

Naomi was angry with her father.

Sev was right and Naomi knew he probably thought her pathetic but she wasn't.

She was here to find out for herself.

Growing up, she had felt like her mother's biggest mistake. Naomi was quite sure that her mother had set out to get pregnant in the hope of saving her marriage and blamed Naomi that it hadn't worked. Her childhood seem to have been spent waiting for the postman or phone calls that had never come.

He had paid child support and her mother had even resented that. Anderson had performed his legal duty towards his daughter and no more.

As a teenager Naomi had once picked up the telephone and called her father out on his shortcomings. He had listened and then listed his reasons for hardly getting in touch over the years.

He'd said that he hadn't wanted to cause friction between Naomi and her mother.

Work was another reason he had given.

Then there had been pressures with his then wife, who hadn't wanted to hear about his daughter in England.

That marriage had long ago broken up and now he was with Judy.

The excuses were running out but Naomi wanted to know for herself. She didn't want to rely on her mother's bitter, jaded opinion of her father.

And that was why she was here to find out for herself if he wanted her to be a part of his life.

Naomi turned on her tablet to read her horoscope, and laughed to herself as she thought about how she had lied to Sev at her interview...about many things.

'Tensions are at an all-time high tonight for all the star signs...' the astrologer warned, and Naomi read how some cosmic event meant that there was friction everywhere and arguments breaking out and, the astrologer advised, if you didn't have firm plans, then it might just be better to stay home.

Naomi rolled her eyes and checked the date.

Surely the astrologer was referring to last night, Naomi thought.

How wrong she was!

Her father and Judy were back just on midnight and, though they didn't shove her out the door when they came in, it was obvious that they would prefer she soon left. Judy kept yawning and saying how tired she was and there was no suggestion that Naomi have one of the brandies that Anderson was pouring and stay the night.

Or maybe she was just a little too used to Sev!

'I'll try and get over before I go to Dubai,' Naomi said as she did up her coat.

'Oh, but you'll be far too busy for that,' Judy said. 'Don't worry about visiting us, we'll still be here when you get back.'

'But it's your fiftieth birthday on Friday, Dad.' Naomi

looked at her father and then back to Judy, and she watched as their false smiles froze.

'How did you know?' her father asked.

'Because I always remember your birthday,' Naomi answered, and struggled to keep the edge from her voice because he hadn't remembered a single one of hers. 'What are you doing to celebrate?'

'Nothing!' Anderson snapped.

Judy guided her out to the hall and had a quiet word. 'He really doesn't want a big deal made about his birthday,' Judy said in a low voice. 'I think it's the middle-aged thing, what with me being so much younger. He just wants it to pass unnoticed so, please, Naomi, don't make a fuss and just leave it. We'll see you when you get back.'

The car was freezing and took for ever to warm up and then she got stuck on the bridge for ages.

Naomi turned on the radio for company and tried to sing along with a song, but who was she kidding? She was crying her eyes out. All she had ever wanted was a family. Parents who cared and said things like, 'Oh, my daughter Naomi is good at that.' Or who passed a shop window and thought, Naomi might like that. Maybe it was why it had taken so long to end things with Andrew. She'd kept hoping he'd turn into the real deal and she could make a family of her own. It hadn't and so she cried and continued to do so all the way back to her apartment. And then, just when the night couldn't get much worse, as she dashed through the foyer, there at the elevators she saw him.

Sev.

And he was standing there, getting very friendly with Felicity, her predecessor.

They both looked stunning. Sev was in a suit and a heavy grey coat. Felicity was all blonde and gleaming and Naomi, wearing jeans and flat boots, felt incredibly drab. She was tempted to turn and wait till they had gone, but that would make it more awkward if she was caught walking off. They were laughing at something but the smile faded from Sev's face when he turned and saw Naomi walking towards them. He dropped Felicity from his generous, given freely and regularly to any suitable female, embrace.

'Hi,' he said by way of an awkward greeting, but then he saw her red eyes. 'Are you okay?'

'Never better.'

It was the most excruciating elevator ride of her life. Felicity kept trying to get off with Sev and rubbing up against him like a cat wanting to be fed, and so when the elevator doors finally opened Naomi practically flew out.

She let herself into her apartment and found that, no, she didn't feel like crying now, she was furious instead.

Felicity!

She knew that he'd slept with her in the past and she knew he had simply gone out and replaced her tonight and not even with someone new.

Lazy bastard.

Hell, yes, she was angry. Naomi stripped off and got into her dressing gown and, rather than thinking of them bonking their brains out a few floors up, she went under the sink and pulled out a bottle of red wine.

New York was possibly the loneliest place in the world, Naomi decided.

It had been when she'd been here at eighteen.

Oh, it was the most beautiful busy city in the world but sometimes she felt as if it could swallow her up and make her disappear and no one would even notice that she had gone.

All she wanted was a home.

And then there was a knock at the door.

She ignored it. Maybe it was next door and they had forgotten where they lived...

There was another knock and then came Sev's voice. 'Naomi, it's me.'

Oh, this she so did not need.

If he'd forgotten his keys he could get the doorman and she'd tell him that.

'It's the middle of the night,' Naomi said, as she opened the door, but then she saw the slap mark on his cheek.

'What happened?'

'Felicity didn't like it when I told her she really needed to understand that when a man says no, he really means no...'

Damn him, Naomi thought, he could still make her laugh.

'She's gone home.'

'Sev, what are you doing here?' Naomi asked.

'I'm out of sugar.'

'No, really.'

'You've been crying.'

'Do I need a permission note for that?' Naomi asked, but instead of closing the door she stepped back and let him in.

'How's Daddy dearest?'

'I don't need another lecture from you, Sev.'

'Maybe you do.'

He looked at her swollen eyelids and red nose. And then he looked down at the wineglass she was holding. 'Is that wise?'

This from a man, Naomi thought, who had sneaked vodka at a dry dinner last night.

'I think I'm entitled to a glass of wine, given the day

that I've had,' Naomi said. 'Believe me, Sev, I've earned this.' She went to take a sip but he took the glass.

'I mean, should you be drinking if you're pregnant?'

Naomi was too taken aback to respond at first.

'Look,' Sev continued, 'I admit that it's taken me a while to get my head around it and I know that I've never had a pregnant PA before, but I'm sure we can work something out. I think there's a baby-minding centre downstairs somewhere and maybe we can look at cutting back on your travel.'

'Sev.' She found her voice. 'Why would you think I'm pregnant? Where on earth did that come from?'

'Isn't that why you're leaving?'

'I thought that I didn't need a reason to leave?'

'You don't. I was just trying to work out why you were,' Sev said, and then he frowned because it certainly wasn't something he usually bothered trying to work out.

People left.

People came and went in his life and he had learnt long, long ago to accept that as fact.

It just wasn't proving so easy to do that with Naomi.

'Why would you think I was pregnant?' she asked.

He chose not to mention the fertility statue in his office. 'Well, you're moody...' he looked back at her eyes '...teary and temperamental, and it's been going on for far too long for it to be PMS...'

'Would you like me to redden the other cheek?' Naomi offered.

'You yourself said that you've lost weight when you thought you should be putting it on.'

'I was referring to the amount I eat.' Naomi started to laugh. 'It's stress.'

'Do I stress you?'

She dodged the answer. 'Not everything is about you, Sev.'

Not quite everything.

'Phew,' Sev said. 'So you're definitely not?'

'Definitely not.'

'Then I think we should celebrate!'

'Celebrate?' Naomi checked. 'Celebrate what? That I'm not pregnant?'

'I can't think of a better reason.'

Clearly Sev was a lot more used to celebrating than she was because, having taken a sip of her wine and screwing up his nose, he promptly rang down to one of the restaurants on the lower level. Despite the hour, very soon there was champagne nestling in a bucket and a delicious platter of hors d'oeuvres that were far nicer than the nibbles that had been left in the fridge by her father and Judy.

He even lit a fire, which Naomi had been too worried to do just in case the apartment filled with smoke.

'I thought it was just for decoration,' Naomi admitted.

'I don't believe in things being for decoration,' Sev said. 'Here's to Naomi not being pregnant.'

'Here's to that,' Naomi agreed.

'How would he take it?' Sev asked, sitting down on the floor by the fire. Not thinking, Naomi joined him.

'Who?' Naomi said, distracted now because he was so bloody smooth they were on the floor by the fire and if she wasn't careful, they could well end up naked.

'Your fiancé?'

'Sev...'

'I'm just asking.'

'Well, I'm not discussing a hypothetical pregnancy that you conjured up.' She shook her head.

God, she was very glad she would never have to find out how Andrew might have taken that news.

It was so nice, though, to sit talking in front of the fire. Sev showed her how he could balance a champagne glass on his stomach, and given hers wasn't quite so firm and she was only wearing a robe Naomi declined when he suggested she try.

Though now she lay on the floor beside him.

It was silly, it was nice and then she remembered where and with whom he'd recently been.

'How was the theatre?'

'It was terrible,' Sev admitted. 'I hate the theatre.'

'You said you loved it when you took me.'

'Well, it was your birthday. If I'd said I hated it you wouldn't have gone.'

She thought back to that time. Not once had she guessed it had just been for her. Sev had said he'd had the tickets for ages. It was quite simply the nicest thing anyone had ever done for her on her birthday.

'Anyway, this one was particularly bad,' Sev said. 'It was all songs.'

'Well, it is a musical.'

'I hate them. Why can't they just talk? Imagine if I sang everything to you?'

She couldn't.

But then she did.

'You know how nice and sweet Jamal is?' Sev asked, and their brains must be hot-wired tonight because he then sang the same line in a deep baritone. 'You know how nice and sweet Jamal is…?'

They started laughing but then Sev, bored with singing, told her what had happened. 'When she realised that I hadn't brought you, sweet Jamal turned into an utter bitch. Honestly, she ignored Felicity and she was downright rude to me. She was even more badly behaved than we were last night and that's saying something.'

Naomi laughed and then she asked something she wanted to know. 'Are you and Allem friends?'

'Sort of.' Sev shrugged.

'How did you meet?'

'A chat room,' Sev said, and he saw her cheeks go pink. 'Not everything is about sex, Naomi. I had an idea for cell phones and, of course, I couldn't afford to do anything with it. I didn't tell him fully what it was but he was curious enough and rich enough to want to know more. He flew me to Dubai and we discussed it. It was odd. When you talk online you just talk business. Only when I got there did I realise he was a rich sheikh and he in turn found out that I was...' Sev shrugged. 'Well, put it this way, I hadn't flown before, let alone first class. A couple of months later he flew me here to work on a prototype. I've never really gone back.'

'At all?'

'A couple of times,' Sev said, but he was more interested in hearing about her.

'So, what upset you tonight?'

'My father and Judy were actually at the theatre.'

'You wish he'd offered to take you?'

Naomi nodded.

'Were he and your mother together for long?'

'They got married when my mum found out she was having me but they broke up when I was a few months old.' Naomi stared at the ceiling and the shadows dancing there. 'I think she got pregnant in the hope of forcing something between them,' Naomi said. 'And then spent the next twenty-five years regretting it.'

'You're not close to her, then?'

'No.' Naomi shook her head. 'She was very career focused. My school holidays I was palmed off to aunts or my grandparents. All I've ever wanted is a family, can you get that?'

He had wanted a family.

Growing up, it had been a secret dream.

A few years ago it had turned into reality but the plump, smiling woman he'd sort of envisaged his mother to be was, in fact, a skeletal alcoholic who wanted nothing to do with him.

And as for his sister!

Yet he had been about Naomi's age when the dream had died and he had realised that a childhood dream was all it had ever been.

'It's a childish want, Naomi.'

From anyone else it might have sounded mean, yet it didn't when it came from Sev.

'You want the dream.'

'I do.'

'You have a family,' Sev pointed out. He looked at Naomi. She was one of the home kids who had stuck rice on a card for their mother. One of the home kids he'd assumed had had everything.

He knew better than that now.

'Accept what is instead of trying to rearrange the formula.'

'It's not maths, Sev.'

'No,' he conceded, 'but maybe if you think of it more logically…'

'Aaaggh.' She banged her feet on the floor.

'Don't let people upset you, don't dwell on things so much.'

'I just want to give me and my father a chance. If you think about it *logically*, he doesn't know me. I'm giving us that chance. It's his fiftieth on Friday.' Naomi sighed.

'They were horrified that I'd remembered and then he and Judy kept telling me not to make a fuss about it.'

'Then don't.'

'I can't just ignore his birthday.'

'Of course you can,' Sev said. 'I do things like that all the time.'

'You're not normal, though.' Naomi smiled. 'What's his name?'

'Anderson.'

'Anderson Johnson?' Sev said, flicking through his mind like some search engine, trying to work out if he'd come across him before, but Naomi shook her head.

'No, my mother gave me her surname.'

'So what's his?'

'Anderson.' Naomi said, and she watched as his lips twitched into a smile.

'His name is Anderson Anderson?' Sev checked, and Naomi nodded.

'Thank God he's only ever had daughters, then…' Sev put on a formal voice. 'Allem, I'd like you to meet Anderson Anderson and this is Anderson Anderson, Junior…'

'Stop it,' Naomi said, though she was smiling.

Lying by a fire with Sev, her wretched night had been saved and she felt happy for once.

'So what's *your* father's name?'

'Pass,' Sevastyan answered. 'And, no, that's not his surname. I mean pass as in can we change the subject?'

She did, but only a little bit. 'What's your mother's name?' Naomi said. 'Am I allowed to ask that?'

'Breta,' Sev answered. 'Next question.'

She guessed he didn't want to dwell on them and so, given that he had invited her to, she asked instead about something else that had been bugging her. 'Why white roses?'

'You prove my point without me having to make it,' Sev sighed. 'Women read far too much into things that need no reading into at all. If I send red, they'd think love, if I send pink then its romance. Maybe I could try yellow, but I'm sure that they'd come up with something... White is just white.'

'Weddings,' Naomi said, and he shook his head.

'Oh, no, not me.'

'Virgins?' Naomi smiled but again he shook his head.

'Not by the time I send flowers.' He turned and matched her smile. 'Why can't women just get that I'm not going to be around for long? I don't want anyone for long.'

She just lay there as he spelt out what she already knew.

'Next question,' Sev said.

Oh, she had so very many questions but she settled for a rather tame one. 'What is your favourite colour?'

He was about to say that he didn't have one but then Sev decided that maybe he did and even if not, his answer might earn him a favour and he stared deeply into her eyes as he answered. 'Brown.'

'Oh, please.' She was so over his chat-up lines.

'It really is.'

'Faded, dried-up roses...' Naomi sighed.

'Lie between pages,' Sev said, and she thought about his words for a moment as she stared into his eyes.

They would lie between the pages, Naomi thought.

If she were ever the recipient of a bunch of roses from him then that's exactly where they'd end up.

'What's your favourite colour?' he asked.

'I don't have one,' Naomi said. 'I once dared to say green when I was sixteen and every year since then my mother buys me a green eye-shadow palette for Christmas.'

'You have to answer the question.'

'Black, I guess.'

'Technically, black's not a colour, it's actually the absence of colour…'

It was, Naomi thought. It was the delicious absence of colour that she would see any moment now, because his mouth was next to hers and when their lips met, black would be all she'd see.

It would be like sinking under anaesthetic, Naomi thought, but then he'd tear out her heart and use it like a stress ball, for a few hours, days, maybe weeks.

Right now she didn't care.

It was the lightest kiss, only their faces moved towards the other, and he tasted every bit as smooth and expensive as she had thought he might. They remained on their backs, eyes open. His mouth was very soft and his kiss tender for a whole six seconds.

He rolled onto his side and took over the kiss, just in case she changed her mind.

Naomi didn't and she saw her favourite colour as she closed her eyes.

Oh, she wished his kiss would disappoint her. How much easier would that make things if it did?

Instead, though, he kissed her harder and his champagne tongue slid in as skilfully as the hand that moved into her robe and straight to her breast that had ached for him since last night when he had suddenly terminated contact and pulled up her zip.

She struggled but only internally. Outside her head her body was utterly willing. Naomi could feel how hard he was against her thigh and from their deepening kiss her prediction was right—they'd very soon be naked on the floor.

'Naomi,' Sev said, as if he'd just struck gold.

He felt as if he had.

Yes, he'd imagined kissing her but they had been clumsy in his imaginings—a kiss to persuade, while this was so sensual and her mouth was just made for him. He moved on top of her, his elbows by the sides of her head. His erection pressed against her and he just looked down at her and pressed in again.

She was on the edge of coming just at that.

And he could feel it, the engine of her just revving, and his hand was down to his belt. Foreplay would have to be afterplay because Sev had to be inside her.

There was a frantic tussle that was deeply sexy. Her hands were trying to get her out of her knickers as he freed himself, and there wasn't even a thought as to protection. Sev even wondered if he'd get it in before he came as her hips pressed up into him.

And then she remembered that had she not come home when she had, he'd be a few floors up with Felicity now.

Sev was right, she would read more into things than she should if they made love.

Made love.

She'd just proved her *own* point without even having to make it.

God, she knew better than that.

It was like being stuck on the runway in Mali, Sev bored, with a few hours to kill and nowhere else to go.

'Stop.'

Oh, there was a word for girls like her, Naomi knew, but she didn't care if she was a tease. She would hold on to her heart and, breathless, still wanting, she halted things.

He looked right into her eyes as she denied him and then he rolled off and Naomi sat up.

He said not a word.

Sev stood and did up his belt and Naomi sat, unable to look up at him.

''Night, Naomi,' Sev said, his voice black. He went to go but then changed his mind and turned around and strode back.

'Is it because of him?' He picked up her hand and examined the ring that she wore as a shield—how foolish to think a bit of gold could protect her from Sev. 'I wouldn't waste too many guilt trips on him. It's a fake.'

She thought he'd rumbled that the engagement was now a fake so it took a second to realise that Sev was talking about the stone in the ring.

Oh, she had so many other things to cry over but right now this would do. Only Sev didn't see the silent trickle of tears on her cheeks, he was too busy examining the ring, and though he didn't usually deal in feelings, he'd just been teased to the brink and he could be as much of a bitch as she.

'Did he get it out of one of those catalogues that you English have?' Sev's grin was malicious. 'Is he paying it off at fifty pence a week for the next twenty-four months?'

'Bastard!'

He was appalled when he saw her tears.

'Do you get a kick out of embarrassing me, Sev?'

'He's the one who should be embarrassed.'

'Will you please just go?'

'You know, I might be a bastard, Naomi, but at least I'm not a cheap one.'

No, Sev was a very expensive bastard, Naomi thought as she took off the ring and tossed it into the fire.

He could cost her her heart.

CHAPTER SIX

THANKFULLY, NAOMI DIDN'T have to see him the next day—whatever he was up to in Washington was classified and so she hadn't been required to go along.

Instead she woke at sunrise and lay in bed, embarrassed and cross with herself for what had happened last night.

Sev had had every right to be annoyed. She had been utterly willing and completely wanting.

She still was.

How could she tell him that it wasn't the sex part that worried her, it was afterwards?

Naomi had come to New York with the knowledge she might have her heart broken by her father. She really didn't need the added pain of Sevastyan Derzhavin and that, as he'd told her last night, was a guaranteed hurt.

She knew the appalling mixed messages she had sent, though, and she owed him an apology at least.

Naomi reached for her phone and then changed her mind.

Not yet.

For now she went into work and got on with the job of trying to find her replacement, as well as attempting to produce a file, as she had when she had left previous employers, outlining Sev's routines and preferences.

He was consistently inconsistent, though.

Even his coffee preferences changed from one cup to the next.

She scrolled through his diary, trying to establish some sort of pattern.

He travelled the world but his journeys were scattered.

The only thing that was regular was that he went to England once a year in November, Naomi noted as she scrolled through his past.

He called her a few times during the day but it was all strictly business. The disaster of the other night wasn't referred to, and though Naomi had a few questions for him they were mainly logistical.

'I don't think you can manage four full days in Dubai if you want to be in London by the eleventh.'

'Just sort it.' Sev's response told her that he'd far rather be concentrating on work than speaking to her.

And so she did her best to sort it and then got on with the first round of interviews for her replacement.

It was harder than she'd thought it would be.

Imagining them here, with him, and herself gone.

'You've interviewed for the role on two previous occasions?' Naomi checked, as she went through Emanuel's excellent résumé late on the Thursday afternoon. Tomorrow was her last day in the office and, despite her best attempts; she had only found one suitable applicant.

Hopefully Emmanuel would make it two.

'I have.' He nodded. 'The first interview went well but Mr Derzhavin was concerned that I didn't speak Mandarin. I do now. I've been attending night classes for two years and I also had a month in China to immerse myself in the language.'

He really wanted this job, Naomi realised, somewhat

startled when she thought of her own poor language skills and how Sev had said they could work around that.

There must be another reason, surely, that Sev hadn't employed Emmanuel, and she would do her best to find out what it was before she put him forward.

'And what happened at the second interview?'

'It never went ahead. I arrived late,' Emmanuel said. 'It's inexcusable at an interview, I know, but my dog had a seizure just as I was walking out of the door.'

'Did you tell Sev that?'

'I never got the chance.'

'And how's your dog now?' Naomi asked, but then wished that she hadn't as the tip of Emmanuel's nose went red and his eyes filled with tears.

'He had to be euthanised.'

Late on Thursday Sev rang to say he was home but could she pop out and get him some headache tablets?

'Why aren't there any?' Sev snapped. He paid for others to deal with these things and all he wanted to do was to go to bed.

'I forgot to check,' Naomi admitted, remembering when she'd done her monthly inventory but had baulked after checking the bedside table.

No, she would not miss this part of her job, Naomi thought as she knocked and then let herself into his penthouse suite.

He looked terrible. He was paler than usual and she could see his exhaustion. Naomi wondered why he was on his computer when surely he needed a break?

'How was Washington?'

'Cold.' Sev shrugged.

'Here are your headache tablets.' She put them down on the desk.

'Do you need anything else?'

'Nope.'

'About my replacement—I've narrowed it down to two applicants. The first interview is at midday. I think they're both—'

'I think,' Sev interrupted, 'that that can wait for tomorrow. I don't want to think about work.'

She let herself out and Sev punched out three headache tablets. No, it hadn't been a ruse to get her to come up. He was tired, had a headache and it was *still* November.

He was checking through his emails.

His mother's care level had been upgraded to high dependency. Another email informed him that the two gifts he had sent his niece had been delivered.

Sev had sent a small gift to Mariya's home but the main one he had sent to her school.

He didn't trust his half-sister at all.

Last year he had sent Mariya an antique necklace. It really had been a stunning piece but then, flicking through an auction catalogue a couple of months later, he had come across it.

The earrings he had bought not just with his niece in mind.

They were a touch more generic.

If she sold them on, he wouldn't know. He really didn't need a reminder as to how he'd been used.

The headache tablets did nothing and he woke the next morning and for a very long while debated whether or not he would even go in to work.

Of course he had to.

He walked and, unusually for Sev, stopped and bought a coffee before heading up to his office.

Naomi was in already, wearing the same suit that

she'd had for her interview, and it certainly wasn't too tight now.

He offered a brief good morning and then went into his office, closing the door. He sat staring at the door, picturing her behind it.

He'd miss her and Sev didn't like that feeling at all.

In fact, he was considering telling Naomi that he would prefer that she leave today rather than come with him to Dubai.

'Who's my first applicant?' Sev asked, when Naomi came in to ask how he wanted his coffee this morning.

'Her name is Dianne,' Naomi said. 'And then you've got Emmanuel at two p.m. They're both excellent'

'I'll decide for myself, thank you.'

'Do you want coffee?'

'I've already got it.'

He nodded to a take-out cup.

It felt like a snub.

It wasn't.

He just wanted it to be over and done with.

Sev sat thinking.

Okay, if one of the applicants was suitable and could start straight away, then he'd suggest that they do just that.

Midday came and Dianne arrived on time and gave Naomi a wide smile.

'He shouldn't be too long,' Naomi offered. 'Can I get you a drink?'

'No, thanks.' Dianne's smile stayed on and she took a seat as Naomi buzzed Sev to let him know the first applicant had arrived.

Naomi did her best not to look up as Sev came out of his office but, having shown Dianne through, he then came out of the office and over to her desk.

'You might as well go to lunch.'

'Sure.'

Naomi wasn't foolish enough to think Sev was going to be taking her out for a little leaving do.

She had hoped he might, though.

How she wished she could erase the other night. Well, not all of it, just the ending.

In fact, she wished now that she had slept with him.

Just to have known what could have been.

More than that, she wanted 'them' back, the little in-jokes, the easy conversation.

Now it was tense and awkward.

His voice was tart and she could barely look up and meet his eyes as he delivered his instructions for the rest of the day.

'Can you make sure my case is packed before you finish? I've got company tonight, I don't want you coming around after five.'

'Of course,' Naomi said. 'I'll go over now.'

'Before I go in…' he nodded in the direction of his office '…how soon did she say she could start?'

'She's available straight away.'

Naomi knew then that she wouldn't be going to Dubai.

Back to his apartment Naomi went.

For the last time, she was quite sure.

There were no maids there. They had clearly been in, though. His bed was made, Naomi noted as she took out his case.

She took out her tablet and pulled up the list she kept for Sev's packing. It would be hot and humid in Dubai and cold, possibly wet in London so she decided to pack a separate case for each. She packed his shirts and suits and a couple of casual options. And then she dealt with his toiletries.

How odd, she thought, that she could have such access to someone's life and still know so little about them.

And this really was it.

Naomi moved the cases through the entrance hall and had one final walk around. She was dreading going back to the office, to be told her services were no longer required.

But it was surely better this way.

She should have followed her instincts three months ago and said no to the job there and then.

Her heart had already known just how hard this would be.

Naomi didn't stop for lunch. Instead she went to the patisserie she had called earlier in the week and picked up the cake she had ordered.

It looked amazing.

A champagne-and-raspberry layer cake and, yes, she stopped and bought a bottle of champagne to go with it.

'Are we having your leaving party now?' Sev asked when Naomi came back from her lunch break carrying the champagne and cake box.

'You didn't need to go to so much trouble,' Naomi quipped.

Sev got up and followed her into the little kitchen where she usually prepared drinks and things for his clients, and when she put down the box he opened the lid and saw 'Happy 50th, Dad'.

'Naomi,' Sev warned. 'He clearly said that he didn't want a fuss.'

'People always say that,' Naomi said, putting the bottle in the fridge.

'Men generally mean what they say,' Sev said. 'Well, bastards do. When they say leave it they mean leave it. Take it from me and don't make a big deal of it.'

'It's just a cake.'

Oh, he knew that it was so much more than a cake.

It was her heart and her hope smeared between the layers and she was going to get hurt, Sev knew.

He knew exactly.

Not that he could tell her that without telling her about himself, which he chose not to do.

Not his problem, Sev decided.

'Everything's ready for Dubai tomorrow. The car's booked for six a.m.,' Naomi said. 'You fly at seven and arrive in Dubai for six on Sunday morning.'

'And I fly out when?' Sev said. He had heard she had taken herself out of the equation, he just had to officially tell her, that was all.

He just wasn't ready to yet.

'You leave Dubai at five a.m. on Thursday the twelfth and with the time difference get into London at eight a.m. the same day.'

'But I said specifically said that I wanted to be there by the eleventh,' Sev pointed out.

'And then you said you needed four full days for Allem and to just make sure you got into London early.'

'Not good enough, Naomi.' The day he hated the most in the world had just been extended by four hours! 'When I say I want to get there on the eleventh, you get me there on that date.'

'I can't rearrange time zones,' Naomi said. 'Believe me, I've tried.' She didn't want things to end on a row. 'I'll go and have another look at it,' she went on. 'If you leave Dubai—'

'Just leave it as is,' Sev snapped.

He hated the eleventh too.

If he could change one date, it would be that one.

He would have asked more questions, pushed for his

friend to speak or just stayed awake and made sure he was okay.

It wasn't a coincidence that Sev had hoped to meet Daniil on the twelfth.

That was the morning he had woken up in the orphanage to find the bed next to him empty. Nikolai's exact date of death was unknown but Sev had hoped, on what he considered the anniversary, to let Daniil know what had been lost that day many years ago.

'How did the interview with Dianne go?'

Sev shook his head. 'She's not suitable.'

'She was perfect.'

'Not for me,' Sev said. 'She had one of those nervous smiles.'

Naomi let out a tense breath but then she thought back and she smothered a smile of her own because, yes, Dianne had. 'Sev, you thought that I said sorry too much, remember? Surely you can give her a chance.'

'Nope.'

'Well, hopefully the second interview goes well.'

'I doubt it, it's his third application,' Sev pointed out. 'Why can't some people get that no means no?' He met her eyes then. 'I do.'

'Sev.' Naomi had never been braver in her life and he looked at her very red cheeks and saw the tears in her eyes. 'I want to apologise for the other night. I backed out…'

'You had every right to.'

And, no, he didn't want things to end on a row either.

He came over and he took her burning cheeks in his palms.

'It's fine.' He could see her tears. 'No crying over me,' Sev said. 'I've been thinking too.'

'About?'

'The catalogue comment.'

He trawled through his very impressive multilingual vocabulary and came up with that little-used word.

'Sorry.'

Naomi gave him a tired nod.

'I never meant to embarrass you. I was just…'

'I get it.'

'Did you give him hell?' Sev asked. He had happily noted she wasn't wearing the ring.

'No comment.'

And he looked into those deep brown eyes and he wanted to know more, he wanted Naomi to say that she'd dumped him.

Why did he need to know?

'Right.' He brought the subject back to work. 'In all seriousness, I'm less than hopeful about the next applicant. He was late last time.'

'Because his dog had a seizure.'

'Well, that doesn't bode well! So, if I employ Emmanuel, then I've got to arrange my schedule around my PA's epileptic dog.'

'He was euthanised.' Naomi sighed. 'Sev, the man's spent the last two years learning Mandarin on your casual suggestion. At least give him a fair go.'

Sev didn't want to give him a fair go.

And, despite his musings this morning, he didn't want her gone.

He loathed that she was leaving.

A while later his intercom buzzed and Naomi informed him that Emmanuel was here. She remembered her first interview with him, standing up and knocking over a glass at her first sight of him.

He still had the same effcct on her. Sev turned her to jelly on the inside.

'Emmanuel.'

Sev's deep, rich voice still entranced her.

And he was still beautiful.

Just that.

Sev gestured with his head to his office and Emmanuel stood, took a deep breath and then followed him in.

'So,' Sev said, 'we meet again.'

Emmanuel interviewed like a dream.

'Why do you keep applying to work for me?'

'I want to work with the best.'

'And are you aware of the hours?'

'Naomi was very thorough—she told me there can be eighteen-hour days.'

'Several in a row at times'

'I'm an insomniac,' Emmanuel replied.

He had an answer for everything.

'When could you start?' Sev said.

'Now.'

'Is that fair to your previous employer?'

'I'm actually between roles,' Emanuel answered. 'I saw that, more often than not, you seem to hire around the three-month mark.'

'Most of my PAs burn out after three months.'

'I'm not like most,' Emmanuel said. 'I've been doing some temporary work in the interim. I wanted the opportunity to explain, in person, why I was late last time.'

'Your dog.'

Sev had enough trouble relating to people let alone grasping pets but, no, he didn't expect the guy to step over his dying dog to get here for an interview.

'How many languages…?' He glanced again at the résumé at the same time that Emmanuel answered.

'Four.'

He should have said *quatre*, Sev thought, remembering how Naomi had answered his question.

It was the only teeny fault he could find.

'Naomi will be in contact.'

Sev sat sulking in his office for the rest of the day and when he came out at five she was putting on her coat, guessing he was about to tell her that her services were no longer required.

Emmanuel had given her a thumbs-up when he'd come out of the office and had also told Naomi when she had first interviewed him that he could start any time.

It was just a matter of Sev telling her now.

'How was Emmanuel?'

'Useless.' Sev shook his head. 'There's a reason I've turned him down twice...' He looked at Naomi's bewildered expression. 'Have you got another job to go to?'

'I've got a couple of things in the pipeline.'

'Have you got somewhere to live?'

He saw her swallow.

'Why don't you stay on till you've got another job or I've got a suitable replacement?'

'No, thanks,' Naomi said.

'Naomi, you haven't been able to get an apartment. I heard you this morning on the phone—'

'I'll be fine,' Naomi interrupted. 'It's not as if I'm going to end up homeless. I've got family here after all.'

It dawned on Sev then that this little dark horse was pushing for Daddy-o to finally step up to the plate. Bingo!

That's what she did!

Sev was finally working her out.

He knew that she'd tried to get fired that morning when he'd called her from the plane and she'd given him attitude—Naomi didn't want the confrontation of resigning.

And she was pushing for her father to be the one to tell her that no, he simply didn't want her in his life.

He watched as she headed into the little kitchenette and came back carrying the cake.

'Do you want me to come to your father's with you?'

Sev saw her blink and so did he—as surprised as she was by his offer.

'Er…why?'

'I don't know.' Sev shrugged. 'I wouldn't mind a drive.'

'No, thank you.'

It was her last time here in this office.

She was walking out on a dream job, and a boss that couldn't be called a nightmare but he certainly woke her up deep in the night.

'Will you be coming back to get your things?'

'I took them all yesterday. Sev, I gave you notice, I've done everything I can to find a replacement…'

'Yep.'

He didn't want her to go.

'I'll see you in the morning,' Sev said, and he watched her shoulders sag briefly. 'I need you in Dubai. You agreed to stay for that—there's a lot of work I have to cram into four days.'

'Of course.' Naomi nodded. 'Have you done my reference?'

'I'll do it.'

He'd been saying that all week. Yes, she may only have worked for him for a short while but Sev's name on her résumé would open doors in her future.

Not that she could stand to think of that now.

Oh, she didn't want to leave but neither could she bear working alongside him and running his love life for even a moment longer.

'Good luck with your father tonight,' Sev said. 'Don't build up your hopes.'

And that was it.

He headed to his desk.

Naomi waited, just for a second. She *had* built up her hopes.

She wanted something from him, something she could keep, just something to show she had mattered a little to him.

He crushed them.

No bunch of flowers appeared, no rummaging in his drawer for a gift.

Sev was back to his computer and he didn't even look up as she walked out of the office.

It was a long and difficult drive through peak-hour traffic.

She wasn't expecting much from her father.

Naomi hoped, though, for coffee and cake, they could keep the champagne, she just wanted a little glimpse of family life.

It was Thanksgiving soon, and he and Judy had made no move to invite her.

And then it was Christmas, and they hadn't made any mention of that either.

Naomi had already bought presents for all of them.

They were wrapped and hidden in her wardrobe, though why she bothered to hide them Naomi didn't know because her father had never been over.

She was tired.

After the cake she would drive back and then pack for Dubai and London.

Naomi wasn't even looking forward to going home.

She'd texted her mother her dates and times and she hadn't even replied.

And as for Andrew…

That hadn't been love.

Naomi had been, she now knew, in love with the idea of being in love, or rather someone loving her.

Andrew hadn't.

He'd controlled.

As for Sev…

Naomi's eyes filled with tears but she blinked them back. As she neared her father's home there were cars everywhere so she parked a bit away and watched as a couple did the same and got out.

They were holding a gift and walking towards the beach.

So were a small family.

'Anderson's so lucky with the weather…'

She just stood there.

And then, when perhaps it would have been wiser just to get back into the car and drive, instead she followed the people heading for the dark beach.

And there, on a cold clear night, were gas burners and music and a party happening.

One she hadn't been invited to.

The seagulls would have the most wonderful feast because she dropped the cake on the sand and turned and ran.

She just ran to her car and reversed it out and drove.

A party and he hadn't even invited his own daughter!

Naomi was too hurt even to cry.

What the hell was she even doing in New York?

CHAPTER SEVEN

How had things gone with Naomi and her father?

As Sev reached over to turn off his alarm, it was the first thought on his mind.

It was only because he knew, better than most, what she might be going through that he was concerned for her, Sev told himself.

He lay for a moment before he got up, thinking about the days ahead. He wasn't particularly looking forward to Dubai but he had put it off for a while.

Allem was always asking him to come, not just to work but for a holiday. His first time there had been Sev's big break and he hadn't really known it at the time.

He remembered getting his first itinerary and seeing that there would be a stopover in London.

Daniil lived near London.

He had written to Daniil and suggested that they meet outside Buckingham Palace on Nikolai's anniversary. Daniil had been adopted by a rich family and now went by the name of Daniel Thomas. Sev had guessed, rightly as it had turned out, that he wouldn't show up.

Why did he still go to London each year?

Why did he still hope that somehow Daniil might appear when logic dictated otherwise?

Last year he had cancelled the flight but at the last minute had changed his mind.

Literally the last minute.

He had made it to Buckingham Palace on the stroke of midday.

Of course his old friend wasn't there.

Sev thought of another flight he had made when the money had started to come in.

He had returned to Russia full of hope at the thought of meeting his mother.

The memory of that was not one he wanted to dwell on and rarely did. Certainly he never spoke about it with anyone else.

That was why he had awoken thinking about Naomi, Sev decided as he hauled himself as he out of bed and into the shower.

He knew *exactly* how it could be.

Apart from the slight date mix-up with the Dubai-to-London dates, Naomi had arranged things well. All that he had to do was shower and dress. He chose black jeans and a top but couldn't be bothered with shaving.

It was one of those cold mornings that gave the first real indication of the harsh winter ahead and Sev sat in the back of the car and closed his eyes, waiting for Naomi to get in.

Usually they met in the foyer but this morning she wasn't there.

'Where's Naomi?' he asked as his driver got in.

'We just put a load in the trunk and they're just bringing down the rest.'

Sev didn't give it too much thought at first as he was used to women having way too much luggage. When he stopped to think about it, though, it was unlike her.

Like Sev, Naomi travelled light.

Then he heard her voice and when he glanced out of the window she was speaking to the doorman and a lot more bags and cases were being put into the trunk. Not only that, there were some very large parcels with Christmas wrapping on a trolley that, from what Sev could make out, Naomi was leaving with the doorman.

Then he watched as she handed over her keys and a large wad of cash.

Sev said nothing as she got into the car.

She was dressed in a smart black dress with black boots and a neat coat and had a small case, no doubt with a change of clothes for Dubai. She had even put on lipstick, yet she was also terribly white with dark rings under her eyes and on the very verge of tears—so he knew her father must have hurt her and badly.

Bastard!

He felt like telling his driver to take them to Long Island where he could happily haul Anderson Anderson out of his bed but, Sev knew, that wasn't going to help matters.

'How was last night?' he asked instead.

She flashed him a look and then shook her head.

'What's going on, Naomi?' Sev asked. 'Why all the cases?'

'You can take any excess baggage out of my wages,' Naomi snapped.

'Naomi?'

'I'm not coming back here,' Naomi said.

'What the hell happened last night?'

'I don't want to talk about it.'

'Tough!' Sev said, but then he decided it might be best to leave it for now. She really did look terrible and, despite the heating in the car, she was shivering. He wanted to pull out a rug and wrap her in it, or to open the bar and pour her a brandy but he could just imagine her comment if he did so at this time of the morning.

Sev also had the strong feeling that if he pushed Naomi to speak too soon she might just get out of the car at the next set of lights and not even come with him to Dubai.

It would be warmer there.

It was another illogical thought but suddenly he wanted her to be warm and lying in the sun.

They would talk on the plane, Sev decided.

She couldn't avoid him there.

One of the very many plusses of owning your own jet was that there were no queues or lines to deal with. Instead they were driven straight onto the tarmac and there stood Jason, the captain and co-pilot, along with Shannon and another flight attendant.

They boarded and the captain briefed him about flying times. Sev nodded and took off his coat and handed it to Shannon.

Naomi did the same but unlike Sev, who went straight to his seat, Naomi still had some work to do—touching base with his flight crew.

'Come and sit down,' Sev called.

'I shan't be long.'

'I said come and sit down.'

They sat face-to-face in heavy leather seats. The engines were already going and the cabin crew were preparing for take-off.

Sev had declined a coffee, he would have one once they were in the air. He looked at Naomi, who was staring out of the window. There was no point trying to talk to her now, Sev decided, so he took out his book.

He couldn't concentrate, though, and looked over at her.

Naomi could feel his eyes on her as she looked out

at the dark sky. They hurtled along the tarmac and then the plane lifted.

She didn't care if he could see the tears filling in her eyes as she looked down at the Manhattan skyline and remembered her first flight here and all the hope that had filled her heart when she had arrived at eighteen, only to be let down.

The same hope had been present the second time around.

What a fool she had been, Naomi thought.

'You will be back,' Sev said.

'For what?' Naomi asked.

Another round of rejection was the last thing she needed.

Coffee was served—white and sweet for Naomi and a long black for Sev with no sugar today.

There were pastries also and Sev was on his second while Naomi was still nibbling the edge of her first and he could wait no longer to find out.

'What happened last night?'

'I've already told you,' Naomi answered. 'I don't want to talk about it.'

'Well, I'm sorry to pull rank but, given you're leaving the apartment with no notice, I think I have every right to know, and furthermore—'

'I have given you notice,' Naomi interrupted him. 'The only thing that has changed is that I shan't be returning to New York after London. And if you're worried about the apartment, that's already been taken care of,' Naomi said. 'I've brought what I could with me and the rest I'm having shipped home. I've cleaned up as best I can behind me and I've left money for it to be serviced.'

They both knew he couldn't give a damn about all that.

'What about the Christmas presents?'

Naomi closed her eyes.

'It's not even December,' Sev pointed out. He couldn't fathom why she'd had them bought, wrapped and ready.

'I like to be organised.'

'You didn't have to get me so many.' He gave her foot a little kick and Naomi gave a pale smile.

He knew they were for her half-sisters.

'Do you want me get someone to deliver them?'

'Please,' Naomi said. 'If my dad or Judy doesn't come and collect them.'

They wouldn't. Sev was quite sure of that.

'Well, your mum will be pleased to see you.'

He watched those lips stretch and not into a smile. They pushed downwards to suppress tears. He wasn't being a bastard, he was trying to gauge her.

'What happened last night?' Sev asked again.

Still she didn't answer him. Instead she went into her bag and took out two headache tablets and swallowed them down. He could see her hand was shaking as she lifted her glass of water.

'Did you get any sleep?' Sev asked.

Naomi shook head. 'Don't worry, I'll have a doze while you're asleep and I'll be fine by the time we get to Dubai.'

'Go to bed,' Sev said.

'I don't think so.'

There was only one bedroom on the plane and she wasn't in the mood for sharing.

'Go to bed,' Sev said again. 'We're going to hit the ground running once we get to Dubai and right now you look like death warmed up. You represent me, remember.'

It was the only way he might get her to comply.

Shannon came to ask what they would like for breakfast but even the quarter of a pastry she'd had already had Naomi's stomach turning.

She really was exhausted to her very bones. Not only had she spent last night packing and cleaning up the apartment, the previous one she'd had little sleep, nervous, not just because she would be turning up at her father's but that it was her last day in the office.

'What are you doing?' Sev's voice was irritated as Naomi pulled out her tablet, clearly about to start work.

'I'm just going through last night's emails for you.'

Sev answered the questions the emails posed with a clipped yes or no. But finally she gave up pretending that she was okay.

'I might actually lie down, if you're sure.'

'Please do,' Sev agreed. 'You're so white you've got me starting to believe in ghosts.'

Her smile was equally pale as she stood. 'I'm sorry about all of this.'

'I doubt you have anything to be sorry about regarding last night,' Sev said. 'Surely you know me well enough to—'

'Know you!' Naomi angrily interrupted. She wasn't cross with Sev, she knew that, but he was human, he was close and unwittingly perhaps he had hurt her too and so he got a glimpse of what she was holding inside. 'I don't know the first thing about you.'

'What the hell do you mean? You've been running my life for the last three months.'

'Oh, I might know your schedule and your pillow preference for hotels but I know nothing about you, Sev. You tell me precisely nothing, so don't expect me to pour my heart out. You have no idea what I'm going through.'

'You don't know that.'

'What would you know about families? You don't even send your mother flowers for Mother's Day…'

'Hey! Hey!' Sev reared.

'Well, it's true—I've been trying to sort out your diary to hand over. You care about no one, Sev, so don't go offering advice.' She couldn't go on…she had said too much already. She turned and headed to the bedroom, deciding she would apologise to Sev later. Right now she was too spent to feel embarrassed or apologetic.

Again.

She looked around the bedroom. It really was amazing. The trim was ebony, like his bedroom at home, and there was a shower and everything. She could be in a luxurious five-star hotel right now rather than miles up in the sky.

Naomi stripped off her clothes and headed for the shower, though more to see if it would warm her up.

It didn't.

Shivering, she wondered what she should wear to get into bed, but was too tired to work it out so instead she climbed naked into the luxurious sheets and lay there, listening to the hum of the engines and willing sleep to come.

She would love to roll over and bury her face in the pillow and sob but, given Sev was outside, that would just have to wait until she was safely in a hotel room.

So for now she lay and stared up into the darkness, dizzy from being so tired and watching fragments of her heart floating in the air and wondering how to put them all back into one piece.

How to start over again, knowing that her father really wanted nothing to do with her.

That wasn't all of it.

How did she move on, knowing that after Dubai she would never see Sev again?

Sev took one look at the lovely breakfast Shannon served him and pushed the plate away.

He had a large cognac instead.

The colour of sad brown eyes.

He should leave her and let her sleep, Sev thought.

He couldn't.

Sev was quite sure that on the other side of the door she was crying.

He reclined the leather lounger and closed his eyes but, no, he couldn't leave her alone.

Naomi heard a knock at the door but he didn't wait for an answer. She turned and looked at his outline as he stood in the doorway.

'I thought the deal was I got to sleep...'

'I just wanted to check if you were okay.'

'I was almost asleep,' Naomi lied.

'Can we talk? Sev asked.

'No,' Naomi said. Then she hesitated. 'I'm sorry for what I said about Mother's Day.'

'You were wrong.' Sev spoke from the doorway. 'I do send flowers. Mother's Day in Russia is at the end of November but I take care of the delivery myself.'

She just lay there.

'Are you blushing?' he asked.

'I've run out of blushes.'

'Come on, Naomi,' Sev said. 'What happened last night?'

She looked at his outline in the doorway and decided it was easier to admit what had happened when she couldn't see his reaction. And so she told him.

'I wanted to find out how he felt about me and if there was anything to build on.'

'And?'

'Now I know.'

Those three little words told him enough so he went over and sat on the edge of the bed. Naomi felt the matress's indent and was about to tell Sev that if he didn't get out of the bedroom she would, but then he took her hand.

'I know how you feel.'

'Believe me, you don't.'

'Ashamed, unwanted, a mistake…'

He'd picked her top three.

Now she cried.

'It's okay,' Sev said, and his other hand held her shoulder.

She didn't think the tears would ever stop.

And she felt embarrassed.

So, so embarrassed.

Not with Sev, not that she'd broken down; she felt embarrassed for her big fat face eagerly smiling at her father. Embarrassed at the secrets they had gone to such lengths to keep, just to keep her away. And ashamed by the looks her father and Judy had given each other as they'd worked out ways to keep her locked out of their lives. 'I thought that when he got to know me…'

'I know.'

'That when he saw me…'

'I know.'

It was himself she had reminded him of at her interview, Sev thought as he held her.

'*How* do you know?' Naomi asked.

'Because it happened to me.'

CHAPTER EIGHT

SEV NEVER TOLD anyone this.

Ever.

It was one of those private pains that for Sev had been better dealt with alone.

He just didn't want Naomi to have to deal with it alone, though, and so he worked out how best to tell her what had happened to him.

'You're right I don't let others know about me very much…well, not the private stuff…'

'I beg to differ—I order condoms for you. I've dumped two women on your behalf…' She tensed at his emotional approach, trying to keep things light, to somehow keep back because, even though she had spent three months wanting to know more, suddenly he felt too close.

It was going to be hard enough already—saying good-bye.

What would it be like to know more about him and then be apart?

'You don't have to tell me.'

'I will, though.' He looked at her sad brown eyes, which had always melted him, and he knew why now.

He had spent his adulthood avoiding feelings yet lately he felt like a Bunsen burner had been turned on under his emotion button and he just wanted her to feel better, or rather not so alone in this.

He lay on the bed beside her, on his back, and unlike in her apartment it wasn't a smooth move. Yes, she was naked under the sheets, but it mattered little. This conversation was way more intimate than sex and the closest he had ever been with another.

Sev turned his head to face her. 'Do you remember when I spoke about the computer in the office at home and you picked up on it?'

'The one at your school?'

'You were right,' Sev said. 'There was an office where I lived. I was raised in an orphanage.'

She just looked back at him.

'I didn't know if I had parents.' He couldn't properly tell her a little without telling her a lot. 'There were four of us who grew up together,' Sev said. 'We were as good as brothers and we spoke about everything but never that.'

'What?'

'That dream, that hope of being a part of a family.'

He saw her mouth move as if she was about to cry again.

'I get it,' Sev said. 'Daniil and Roman were twins and so, though we were all close, they were true brothers. Then there was Nikolai and I. He felt like my twin—we were the other person in the other's world and we looked out for each other. All four of us said that we didn't care who our parents were and that we didn't care if no one chose to adopt us. I said it all the time but I know I was lying and, looking back, I guess that they were too. Daniil finally did get adopted. He said he didn't want to go but, I'm sure, only because it meant leaving Roman.'

'They split up the twins?' Naomi asked, and Sev nodded but he tried not to dwell on it and to tell Naomi only what was relevant.

'Before that, though, I was good at reading and I would read stories to them at night. We laughed at them but in my head my mother *was* a princess and it was safer that we were apart. Well, I thought that till I was about seven. Then I decided my parents were poor and couldn't afford to feed me but they cried at night for me, or at least on my birthday. I would make up in my head that they were waiting till they could afford to come and get me. I made up so many reasons as to why we were kept apart.'

'I did that too,' Naomi admitted, and she rolled onto her side and faced him. 'I thought it was distance, or work pressure. And he fed me excuses as well—that it was my mother's fault, or his wife who stood in the way…' She looked into Sev's lovely grey eyes.

'A few years ago I found my mother. She had worked as a prostitute and was in a home. I also found out I had a half-sister called Renata, who was quite bit older than me. I didn't know what to do.'

'You didn't know whether to make contact?'

He could see the confusion in her eyes and he knew he had to explain better, and that meant going back, which he hated doing.

'Sev?'

'Okay,' he sort of snapped, but he was actually having to drag it out and make himself out a fool. And then he remembered her tears—the thick, heavy tears she had shed—and he pushed on.

'You think I am rude and antisocial?'

'I wouldn't say that exactly.' He could be a little too social at times, but she gave him a small nod because, yes, he could ignore the niceties at times.

'Well, had you known me a few years ago you wouldn't

hesitate to answer that question. I lived in an orphanage till I was fifteen, then a boarding school, which was hell if you were on a scholarship. So I'd always go to my books and computer. Then I went to university and my room was a quarter the size of this. I studied maths and the people I studied with were the same. I got an internship and was doing really well, but I still rented a room in a house with five guys who were as computer crazy as me.'

Naomi frowned, unsure where this was leading.

'We didn't talk much, we didn't eat together. On weekends I'd go to a bar and hook up, which was the best bit of the week. On the Monday it all started again. Then one day I got an offer to go to Dubai to discuss a design.'

'Allem?' Naomi checked, and he nodded.

'I'd never flown before and Allem flew me first class.'

'Wow!'

'No,' he corrected. 'It was excruciating for me. The whole trip pushed me out of everything I had ever known. I had never eaten with a family before or received a gift but Allem and I did get on and he taught me a lot of things. And so when I found out I had a family I went to Allem. He is good with his family so I asked his advice. Allem said not to be too pushy, to take a gift and some flowers, to understand my mother might be embarrassed or upset at first. I did everything I could to make our meeting go smoothly. I asked the staff at the home to tell her I was coming so that it wouldn't be a shock and then I turned up on time.'

'What happened?'

'I was nervous.' He took her hand and placed it on his chest. 'Thump-thump-thump,' Sev said, at a rate far more rapid than his current heartbeat. 'I walked in and

I was surprised. She was very thin and for the first time I saw someone who looked like me. I recognised her.'

'How old were you when you went to the orphanage?'

'Two weeks old, yet I felt as if I recognised her and I'd never felt that before in my life. I forgot to be calm and I went to embrace her but she pulled back.' He thought about that moment for a while and then he told her the rest. 'She looked at me and said, "I didn't want you then and I don't want you now."' Sev looked at Naomi and said it in Russian just so she could try those words on for size. 'Then she must have seen the suit and the flowers and the gift I had bought and she asked if I had money, which I did by then. Now she is in a nicer home and drinks better vodka but she didn't want me then and she still doesn't want me now.'

'Maybe she—'

'No.' He would not make up excuses or fairy tales again. Never. 'Do you know what? I'm grateful for those words. I really am because I knew there and then where I stood and it would seem that you know now too.'

Naomi nodded.

'It's better to know than to dream.'

'I don't know if I agree.'

'What happened last night?' Sev asked again, and now she was ready to tell him.

'When I got there I saw people heading to the beach and I saw that they were having a party for his fiftieth.' Naomi said. 'I just dropped the cake and ran.'

'Did they see you?'

'No.' Naomi shook, not in answer to the question, more in confusion. 'I don't know, maybe it was a surprise party and—'

'No.' He would not let her have hope. 'If it was a surprise, why wouldn't his wife have asked you to come?'

'Stop it.'

'You need to be tough,' Sev said. 'You need to worry only about yourself from now on.'

'Is that what you do?'

'Absolutely.' Sev nodded. 'I don't care for anyone, I don't *want* to care for anyone, and I don't want anyone ever to rely on me.'

'So you don't care for your friends?' She didn't believe him. 'What about Allem?'

'Oh, Allem says that he wants to be friends and all this talk about me coming for a holiday and taking us out on the water...' Sev shook his head. 'He wants me to call him more and to talk about things other than work.'

'Yet you don't?'

'Not really. He's married now, things are different. I ask after Jamal and I go out to dinner...' he nudged her '...even the theatre, but I know it will change again. Come March they will have the baby. Just stay back from people, Naomi.'

'I'm not like that.'

'Become like that, then,' Sev said. 'I work on it. Sometimes I get drawn in, but I generally choose not to.' He looked at her. 'Take only what you need from people and give no more than you're willing to lose.'

'That sounds selfish.'

'No, it's not. I don't care for family, or deep friendship. I don't want romance and sex is still the best part of my day or week.'

'People get hurt,' Naomi said, thinking of the tears of some of the women she had dealt with but more thinking of herself. 'That's what I was worried about when I said no to you.'

'What? That I was going to turn into some raging monster?'

'Emotionally hurt,' Naomi sighed. Sev wasn't even from Mars, more like the next galaxy.

'From the start I make it very clear sex is all I want. As I said, only gamble with what you're prepared to lose. You *can* choose not to throw your heart in the ring. Expect nothing from anyone...' he gave her a smile '...while demanding excellent service.'

'I don't get it.'

'Take your father, for example. Tell him that if he wants a relationship with you then he has to be the one to make a continuous and sustained effort.'

'But he won't.'

'Then you know.'

'I might never see my sisters.'

'So?'

'I don't want to be like that.'

'It hurts less,' Sev said. 'Call him now and tell him you're gone and tell him why and then see what happens. Do it now—I'll be beside you. Grow some balls, and if you think you can't then borrow mine...' He took her hand and led it to his, and he did so without thinking.

They were on a bed together and he took her hand and placed it there and then he muttered something and went to push her hand back.

Naomi kept it there.

'I didn't come for that,' Sev said.

'I know.'

'I was just making a point.'

'I get that.' Yet her hand remained.

He was semi-aroused, she could feel that.

So was she.

That little trip for Naomi had happened not by the guidance of his hand but earlier, when he had been talking about not throwing your heart in the ring. Naomi had lain there listening but her mind had wandered too. A part of her regret for the other night was that she'd denied herself also.

She wanted Sev, she wanted those lips back on hers, and to give in to the want that had never left since the day they had met.

Could she, as Sev had suggested, take her heart out of the ring?

And as her hand moved over his crotch, Sev conceded to himself that, even though he hadn't come in for that, he had become turned on, which was why his hand had led hers there. Not consciously, more just a natural extension of the feeling between them.

'Naomi,' Sev warned as she continued to explore him. 'I won't let it go down a third time.'

'Third?' Naomi frowned.

'You were hot and naked under those sheets that morning when I called you from Rome,' Sev said. 'Do you want me to remind you of the second time?'

'No.'

'I'm not making a move on you again,' Sev said, and she felt him harden further to her touch. 'You want it, Naomi, then you come and get it.'

He was the most arrogant person she had ever met. He slapped her hand away and sat up, but only long enough to take off his top, which he threw down on the floor, and then lay back.

She had seen the top half of his body many times, usually when he wore a face full of shaving cream, but now he was very unshaven and he lay on his back, looking up at the ceiling, and that body was hers to explore.

If she so chose.

No kiss.

No turning towards her.

No making this easy.

'I mean it,' Sev warned. 'You can make the moves now.'

'What, you're just going to lie there?'

'Yep,' Sev said. 'I've tried being nice and look where it got me. It's your turn to seduce me.' He stretched and closed his eyes. 'If not, I'm going to sleep.'

Naomi lay there on her side and looked over and conceded that she had probably used up rather a lot of chances with Sev.

She went to his mouth and kissed him but Sev did not kiss her back. It was a surprising turn-on, just working his relaxed mouth, tasting cognac at 7:00 a.m., and he was as bad as he was delicious.

Naomi kept waiting for him to reach for her, to respond, but he didn't, he just allowed her to do what she would.

It was an incredible turn-on and she kissed him deeper, sexier, using her tongue to try and get him to respond, but only the deeper breaths from Sev gave any indication of a response.

Two indications, Naomi amended as she knelt back on her heels and planned her next move. She could see him straining beneath the denim and this time *she* went for his belt.

He made it about sex.

Just about sex.

It was incredibly freeing.

And to see this once apologetic person relaxed in herself was surprising for Sev.

When he opened his eyes there was just enough light in the dim cabin that he could see her feminine outline. Combined with the recent feel of her naked breasts on his chest, he was fighting himself not to reach out and touch her.

He loved the bold her.

She dealt with the belt and zip and her hand slid in, feeling him hard and waiting, and his silken pubic hair made her throat close up. Naomi tugged at his jeans and Sev rebuked her.

'I was going to do you fast that night,' Sev said, lifting his hips just enough so she could strip off the bottom half of his clothes.

He gave her nothing except his deep voice but it was more than enough to turn her on, especially as he was naked now and fully erect. He was talking to her in a way she'd never heard. Oh, she'd had the odd reprimand, they had occasionally tipped into a row, but now it ended in bed.

'I was going to take you fast and then I was going to make up for the lack of foreplay…but you said no, that I had to go.'

'Okay…' She didn't need reminders but maybe she did because she was rocking on her heels as she took him in her hand.

'And,' Sev continued his sensual berating of her, 'you think I just wanted a quick come when I was on the phone that time, but then you've never been spoken dirty to by me. You have no idea what you missed out on that morning…'

He said something in Russian, something filthy. It had to be, because her hand tightened her grip on his cock and she tightened inside. Naomi was possibly following orders, because she was climbing on top of him to sit on his thighs.

'Condom,' Sev said. 'Then I want you to get on and…' He switched back to Russian and Naomi, a touch fran-

tic, reached for the bedside table but, no, she didn't deal
with his in-flight toiletries!

'Where?'

'By the shower.'

'You're a bastard, Sev.'

'Yeah, but you're going to go get them,' Sev responded.
'And put the light on on your way back.'

He didn't make her beg; he made her eager.

Sev made her want of him clear because she stood in
the bathroom and saw a face in the mirror that had forgotten tears. She had never seen herself wanton. Naomi
located the necessities and was back in a matter of seconds with her breath coming too rapidly.

'Lights,' Sev reminded her just as she reached the bed,
which meant she had to turn around.

'Walk slowly,' he said, once she had turned the lights
on and his eyes feasted as she did so. He could see how
aroused Naomi was. Her face was flushed, her nipples
erect and her eyes, when they met his, were glittering.

There was such a prickle of anticipation from her head
to her toes that when she touched his cock, she thought
there might be a spark of electricity, but instead it was
warm and moist, only not moist in the way Sev wanted.

'Wet it first,' Sev said.

'I thought I was the one doing the work.'

'Do as you're told.'

She laughed, at herself, at any thought that Sev had
come in here to make love to her, and it helped that this
was not what that was.

She lowered her head, knowing it would be sexual
bliss. Taking charge once more, he positioned her so that
she straddled his face. He didn't touch her, or reach to
taste her, but that only served to incite her desire. She
was moaning to the taste of him, the need for the inti-

mate touch of him which he persisted in denying. Then, as she took him deeper into her mouth, he pulled at her hips and halted her again.

'Turn around.'

He, rather than the motion, made her feel dizzy.

She sat on his thighs, giddy and more turned on than she had thought it possible to be.

Sev tore open the wrapper and held it out to her. 'Put it on.'

'Are you going to say no to me at the last moment?' Naomi wondered aloud.

'Why would I say no to you?' Sev asked, watching as she rolled the condom down his thick length. 'Now get on.'

Oh, he was more than making sure that yes meant yes.

Naomi went to do that. She lifted her hips and he suddenly spun her around and pinned her on her back. Now Sev was on top.

And they were back, exactly where she had said no to him, except they were naked and he was sheathed.

Naomi was arching into him and, just as she had been that night, about to come.

'Oh, no, you don't,' Sev warned. 'You don't get to come without me…' He drove into her, right into her orgasm, and she had never known anything close to it. To be taken so strongly while already coming.

She couldn't even cry out as all her energy gathered around him and the only part of her brain that worked was begging for him to come but he didn't. Sev thrust into her with such intensity that even as her come receded it never fully left. Her life felt as if it had been pale till that point. Naomi's lungs remembered they were supposed to be breathing and she dragged in some air and then found her mouth near his ear.

'Sev...' There was almost a need for him to stop—his rapid, deep thrusts were so consuming, but then he moved up onto his elbows and slowed down but it was no less intense.

Slow and deliberate motions that kept her in this tense sense of gridlock, with an open road ahead, but then, when her urgency increased, so did Sev's speed and he brought her back to boiling, at his whim.

'There,' he said, as he started to come.

'*Krasavitsa*,' Sev said, as he reached his climax, and Naomi let out a shout of pleasure. The lights seemed to go out in her head as he took her to a place she had never been.

Yet he was there with her.

'I think,' Naomi said, as he collapsed on top of her and they lay breathless, 'that you just took my virginity.'

He laughed, understanding that, until now, possibly she hadn't had such sex before.

'I think,' Sev said, 'that you just took mine.'

CHAPTER NINE

'WHAT HAPPENED TO the others?'

They had slept a little, spoken a bit and filled the remaining time with the other. Now, a couple of hours from Dubai, her head felt clearer than it had in three months yet she was curious to know more.

'No idea.' Sev shrugged.

'Have you looked them up?'

'Why?' Sev's voice was scathing. 'So we can speak about happy times?' He relented a touch. 'Daniil is some big-shot businessman now. I wrote to him once but he never got back to me.'

'Roman?'

'I don't know. He was always in trouble, especially after Daniil left for England. I just focused on school and getting the grades so I could get a scholarship and get the hell out of there.'

'Nikolai?'

'Dead,' Sev said. 'When he was fourteen he threw himself in a river.'

There was no elaboration, no emotion, he just told her how it was.

'Why?' Naomi asked, but Sev didn't want to talk about that.

Shannon buzzed and asked if they wanted breakfast.

To Naomi's embarrassment Sev said yes and a little while later she sat up as Shannon brought it in.

Champagne and orange juice was very nice but what made Naomi tear up was a cake and it had her name on it.

'I hadn't told Shannon I was leaving.'

'I called her yesterday.'

So he had made an effort.

'This is your leaving party,' Sev said. 'Though I didn't think we'd be eating it in bed. I'm very glad that we are.'

'We could have done this on the way to London,' Naomi said, but Sev shook his head.

He'd be in no mood to party on the way there, whether or not they were in bed, as it would still be November the twelfth.

He looked at Naomi.

There would soon be another reason to loathe that date.

'Do you have a job to go to in London?'

'My old boss emailed me a couple of weeks ago to say that his current PA isn't working out. I dismissed the idea at the time…' She looked at Sev. 'What you said about working for you still…'

'Naomi.' Sev was as blunt as he needed to be. 'It would be very foolish to come back to New York because of what happened today.'

'I know it would.'

It felt strange to be so honest and to speak with some-one who was so direct. And yet, again, words that might cause offence when said by others didn't when they came from Sev.

She knew where she stood. Or rather where she lay.

'I think,' Sev said, 'that when we get to Dubai you should ring Emmanuel.'

'I thought he was useless?'

'He'll do,' Sev said. He certainly wasn't going to tell Naomi he had only said that in the hope she might stay.

Yes, he didn't want her gone, but for her to return solely for him, Sev knew, would be cruel.

'Do you know what you need?' Sev asked.

'What?'

'A holiday.'

'If I want my old job back I'll probably have to start straight away. I might see if I can take a few days, though.'

'No, I mean a proper one. How about we have a holiday before you go back to London? Both of us?'

'We're going to be busy.'

'No, we're not.'

'You told Allem that you're going to have to squeeze two weeks' work into four nights.'

'That's just so I can bill him adequately.'

'But the work still has to be done.' Naomi frowned.

'Most of it already has been.' He looked at her and smiled. 'Can you keep a secret?'

'Yes.'

'It will take me a couple of days… And before you say I'm overcharging, I'm not. He's paying for my knowledge, not the actual labour. And,' Sev added, 'I'd end up with far too many clients if I didn't pace things. So,' he said, 'how about it.'

'A holiday?'

'A proper one,' Sev said, and then he gave her another tiny glimpse of insight. 'I've never had one before.'

He'd travelled the world many times over and yet he'd never taken a break.

'I don't know…'

'Think about it,' Sev said, and got out of bed and went to the shower.

Naomi did think about it.

She had been scared that if she slept with him she might fall deeper and, of course, she had.

Only she wasn't scared now.

Naomi was sure of her feelings for him.

Oh, it would be a very foolish woman to expect more from Sev.

It didn't stop her wanting more, though.

And some might consider her foolish for upending her life to give herself and her father a chance, but even if it hadn't worked out, she was glad that she had.

'How about it?' Sev asked, as he took the towel from his hips and started to dry his back while facing her.

'How about what?' Naomi smiled.

'The holiday.' Sev grinned. Really, she was nothing like he'd thought she'd be, and he had thought about it a lot!

'Oh, that!' Naomi just lay there looking at him, but her mind was already made up.

No, she wouldn't throw her heart in the ring and she would hold back but, yes, she would open it up enough for potential hurt. There would be no declarations of her feelings and no asking Sev for more than he was prepared to give.

And she would walk away with her head held high.

At least she would have given them a chance.

'I need an answer.' Sev was still drying himself.

'Yes, please,' Naomi said, looking at his hardening manhood. She laughed as he threw down the towel and got back into bed.

'I wasn't asking about that!'

CHAPTER TEN

DUBAI WAS, AS PROMISED, humid and hot, but they were whisked straight from the plane to a stunning hotel complex that was icy cool and very elegant.

Allem proudly showed them around.

It was beyond luxurious.

There were private beaches and pools and Naomi could only guess what the rooms must look like.

'We host a lot of foreign delegates as well as royalty,' Allem explained. 'I never want their privacy or safety to be compromised as has happened at some other hotels. Last month one of our main rivals had their accounts system hacked into,' Allem told Naomi. 'Some very personal information was revealed, which is why I have been pushing for Sev to come and update all our systems. While I employ the best IT staff, I would prefer—'

'It will be fine,' Sev interrupted. 'I'll meet with them but I'll check it myself.'

It was clear Allem really only trusted Sev to have full access to everything.

'I'll return on my way back from London so if there are any glitches I can work on them then.'

'We'll see you both again.' Allem beamed but Sev shook his head.

'Just me. Naomi has resigned. I'll have a new PA,

but he shan't be starting for a couple more weeks. Any problems, just contact me directly, Allem.' He glanced over at Naomi. 'I'll be fine now. I'm going to meet with the IT team. I should be back around two. Just take the day and relax.'

'I hope you will enjoy your stay,' Allem said, 'and I trust that you both will be comfortable. Anything at all that you need, just say.'

'Thank you.'

He stood there as she walked off.

'Why did Naomi resign?' Allem asked.

'I've no idea,' Sev admitted.

He still didn't know. Yes, sex might make things awkward in the end but they were far from awkward now.

'You're finishing at two?' Allem checked.

'I decided to have a bit of a holiday, that's why. If anything doesn't get done, I'll be back after London. It will give me a few days to tweak things as well.'

'You must let Jamal and I show you around. We can go out on the water—'

'No, no,' Sev interrupted, and made no apology for turning down Allem's kind invitation. 'We're just going to relax. Naomi might be starting a new job pretty soon.'

'Oh, so you're both having a break? I see that Naomi is no longer wearing her ring,' Allem commented.

'No.'

'I've put you in adjoining suites.' Allem had remembered Sev's request from the last time he had been there.

Sev liked company.

Just not all the time.

Times, though, had changed.

'No need for adjoining suites,' Sev said. 'Move Naomi into mine.'

By the time Naomi had arrived at Reception, Allem

had made a call and, unknown to her, the arrangement had already been made.

Naomi was checked into a room that was more sumptuous than any she had ever stayed in, or could even had imagined staying in.

The furnishings were amazing, from Persian rugs to vases filled with exotic flowers.

The Persian Gulf stretched out before her and there was an alfresco area with its own pool and spa.

And then she found out why. This wasn't Sev's PA's suite, she realised as the cases she had packed for Sev were delivered and the contents put away, and it was a little closer than she had expected him to be over the coming days.

They had travelled together a lot.

It felt strange, knowing that there wasn't a door that could be closed between them, and for the first time since making her decision Naomi had doubts.

This *was* going to hurt.

She did her best to push their imminent parting out of her mind.

For an hour or so she dealt with work but then she looked through one of the brochures in the suite and decided that, no, they would not be eating in a restaurant tonight and made some reservations.

It was her holiday too!

She enjoyed a morning at the spa and was lying on a vast bed, looking out at the Persian Gulf, when the door opened around three and Sev came in. 'It took longer than I thought but his guys will be working on it round the clock tonight and I'll be back onto it tomorrow. For now we can relax.'

'I thought that we'd have separate rooms.'

'Why?'

'I just did,' Naomi said. 'Come on, you need to get changed.'

'Why?'

'We've got a date with the desert. Camel riding, a meal and belly dancing, and then star-gazing till midnight.' Naomi smiled. 'My treat.'

'You're kidding me?'

'No.' Naomi shook her head. 'I'm not.'

'I don't do that sort of stuff.'

'Well, I want to.'

'Allem will arrange a private tour—'

'I told you,' Naomi said, 'this is my treat. If you don't want to go, that's fine. I think the transport drops us back here about one. I wanted to book the overnight trip but I wasn't sure what time you'd have to work tomorrow.'

It turned out to be the nicest, maddest, most beautiful thing that either he or Naomi could have done.

The desert was stunning, especially looking at it as you rode a camel. The group they were in made a lazy procession as the sun slid down the sky and it was like being bathed in liquid gold.

The magic didn't end there. They arrived hungry at camp to the smoky scents of dinner. They sat on rugs and ate, and their group were all amazing. Some were backpackers, there was a couple on their honeymoon and another here for their wedding anniversary. The shisha pipe came around and Naomi had her feet painted with henna as she ate the best dates she had ever tasted. Then they watched the belly dancing and, as Naomi had known it would be, it was wonderful.

Sev thought so too.

Usually his view was an office, or hotel window, or looking out from his plane.

Now he breathed in the warm night air and that night,

amongst strangers, they lay on their rugs and looked up at the stars as a guide pointed out constellations and star clusters.

'That was amazing,' Sev admitted afterwards, as they still lay looking up at the stars. 'Emmanuel won't be nearly as much fun.'

'He might be once he's resigned.' Naomi smiled and looked at him.

'Did you call him?'

'Yes,' Naomi said. 'He's completely thrilled. He offered to come out to Dubai to transition…'

'You said no to that, I hope. I know the bed at the hotel's big but I'm not sharing with him too!'

'I said no, that there's no need for him to come here at this stage, though you might want him after London.'

'No.' Sev didn't want to think about London, or the trip back here afterwards.

'Anyway, I said that I'd be in touch with dates shortly.'

And Sev got back to looking at the stars. He knew then that she was leaving for sure.

Naomi wouldn't change her mind and come back and work for him; she simply wouldn't do that to Emmanuel.

'What about your father?' Sev asked. 'Did you call him?'

'No.'

All too soon it was over and Sev actually wished that Naomi had booked the overnight trip. They headed back to the hotel and it would seem the fairies had been in while they'd been out—a sunken bath had been run and there were petals floating on the surface of the water. The lights were dimmed and there was champagne on ice. Even Sev blinked.

'I think we've got the honeymoon suite.'

They had.

And, yes, it was like a honeymoon.

Except at the end of it they would be parting ways.

Over the next few days Sev worked harder than he ever had just to give them more time to do the things Naomi wanted to do, like parasailing, long lazy lunches and dinners taken on the beach, and slow walks afterwards.

The moon was so big and yellow, as they walked, that it almost looked like the sun had stayed up too long.

'I called my father,' Naomi told him. 'I just wanted it over and done with.'

'And?'

'I didn't say I knew about the party. I just said that I hadn't been able to find a new job or somewhere to live and so I thought it might be better to stay in London rather than come back.'

'What did he say?'

'That he was sorry we didn't get a chance to say a proper goodbye. I honestly don't know if he meant it.'

She looked at Sev and wondered how their goodbye would be.

'I'm going to stay in touch with my sisters, though.'

'Why?' Sev asked.

And she looked at a man who just didn't care and wondered when her heart would get the message—he never would!

'Did you ever contact your sister?' Naomi asked.

'Yes,' Sev said. 'Renata. She's ten years older than me, a single mum with a daughter...'

'Your niece?'

Sev shrugged.

'I guess.'

'Don't you care about them?'

'Nope.' He saw the flash of confusion in her eyes, and

he was damned if he'd tell her why. 'You rely on others for your happiness too much, Naomi. You just hand out that heart and you wonder why it comes back broken. I'll tell you what happened. I did look up my sister and I was welcomed into their home and I met my niece, Mariya. Then I came back to New York and for a couple of months we spoke most weeks. Then I got a phone call. Renata told me that Mariya was sick, very sick with a very rare form of cancer.'

'Sev!' Her eyes actually filled up. She might not know her sisters well but with the thought of one of them being so ill and so far away, she could understand his pain.

'I was devastated. I'd only just found a family and I asked if there was anything I could do. Renata told me about a treatment that was available in America. It was Mariya's only chance…'

He could see the concern in her eyes.

'She only had a few weeks to live. She was too weak to come to the phone. I offered to pay for the treatment, to bring her over to America. I was going to send the jet and sort out medical team to fetch her but…'

He looked into those spaniel eyes that would trust in others for ever, no matter the hurt they caused, and when Sev hesitated, she assumed the logical conclusion.

'It was too late?'

The logical conclusion if you had a warm heart.

His had grown cold for so many reasons.

'Hey, a bit of advice, Naomi, never, ever respond to an email asking for your bank account details.'

'I'm not with you.'

'I asked Renata for the clinic's name so I could send funds.' Naomi still frowned and it annoyed him. It scared him just how much she trusted and how easily she could be hurt.

Had been hurt.

Could very easily still be.

'Renata wanted me to send the funds directly to her.'

Naomi swallowed.

'Mariya was never sick,' Sev explained. 'There never was any cancer. So you see now why lying about a family member's health comes easily to me. It must be hereditary.'

'You're sure it was a scam?'

'Quite sure,' Sev said. 'I now have nothing to do with Renata but I've sent gifts for Mariya, though they end up auction sites.' He was brutal then. 'Don't go looking for hurt, Naomi. It's the best advice I can give.'

'We're not all like that, Sev.'

'I'm not talking about women,' Sev said, thinking she was referring to his mother and sister, but Naomi was one step ahead of him.

'I know you're not,' Naomi responded. 'You've ruled out the entire human race.'

CHAPTER ELEVEN

SEV STILL HAD to work but, Allem noted, he looked more relaxed than he had ever seen him. 'What are your plans for London?' Allem asked, as Sev took him through the changes he was making to the system.

'Just…' Sev shrugged. He never told anyone that he went there in the hope of catching up with Daniil.

'Will you be meeting Naomi's family?'

'No. Allem, Naomi and I aren't going anywhere.'

'But why not? It's clear you two have strong feelings for each other. It was obvious at dinner but it's fact now.'

'Can we just concentrate on work?' Sev snapped, but for once it was Sev who was distracted.

Sev dealt in facts and Allem was right.

Their walk on the beach and what Naomi had said about him mistrusting the human race had rattled him. Sev knew he had many reasons not to trust in others, except none of them applied when he thought of Naomi.

Tomorrow would be their last full day in Dubai. They had spent the morning in bed and then the pool and Sev, who was usually only too happy to head into work, hadn't wanted to leave her. The day after tomorrow they would be boarding his jet and then Naomi would be gone. There was a part of him that was relieved—he would

restore factory settings on his heart and get the hell on
with his life.

'Jamal and I knew within a week of meeting each
other that we would be together. Our families weren't
happy about it at the time but I knew that she would be
the woman I would marry.'

'Allem,' Sev warned. 'We don't all want a wife.'

'Sevastyan—'

'Leave it.'

'I don't want to leave it. Why would you not fight
for her?'

This, Sev thought, was the reason he didn't want
friends. He had boundaries and Allem was overstepping
them, and it needled at him.

'Sevastyan.' Allem said again. 'How long have we
known each other?'

'Long enough,' Sev said through gritted teeth.

Allem did not take offence.

Oh, he had taken offence when they had first met.
Many times.

Most people, when they stepped off a first-class flight,
would be pleasant and relaxed.

Sevastyan had arrived in Dubai looking grey.

He had refused basic pleasantries and had struggled
through a lavish meal that had been prepared and then
he had, on retiring, put outside the door, unopened, the
gift that had been placed in his suite.

Yes, Allem had been offended.

He had knocked to enquire if the gift did not suit this
very difficult guest.

'Do you remember when I knocked on your door and
asked why you had placed the gift outside your suite?'
Allem asked.

Sev actually let out a low laugh at the memory.

'You thought it had been placed in the wrong room.'

'Because I'd never had a gift.'

'And then you asked if we could get out?' Allem reminded him. 'We went for a drive and to a bar.'

Sev stopped smiling when he remembered that night.

He had never been out of Russia before. The flight had been awful, the constant attention from the flight attendants had unsettled him. Then he had got to Allem's and he had never been a guest in someone's home, especially such a palatial one, and he had been completely overwhelmed.

They had ended up in a bar, one that was far nicer than the ones Sev had been used to frequenting.

'You told me that night where you had come from.'

'Allem,' Sev pointed out, 'I've come a long way since then.'

'You have,' Allem agreed. 'Through your own hard work.'

And some help from a friend. Yes, Sev admitted then that Allem was one.

'Allem?'

Sev gave up trying to work.

He had a question.

Several, in fact.

CHAPTER TWELVE

DUBAI, NAOMI DECIDED, was amazing.

Or was it that she was on holiday?

Her job meant that she had seen many beautiful places but these past couple of days had been so relaxing, exhilarating and wonderful.

Or was it the company?

She didn't try to work it out.

She woke mid-morning to a note from Sev telling her he would be working with Allem till late to give them a clear day tomorrow.

Their last day.

No, she didn't want to think about that and so she had a lazy breakfast in bed, going through brochures and trying to work out, from the many choices available, just what to do with her day. Just when she had decided on shopping she took a call from Jamal, who said it was her turn to take Naomi out.

Naomi found herself laughing as she got ready, thinking back to the day she had met Jamal, when she had been priming herself to hand in her notice.

So much had changed in that short space of time and so much would change again very soon.

'Allem just called,' Jamal said as Naomi got into the

car, as arranged. 'They will be working till late, which gives us plenty time.'

Oh, Jamal knew how to shop.

And her driver patiently took her purchases back to the car.

They went into several boutiques, though Jamal steered away from the names Naomi knew. 'I dress more traditionally,' Jamal explained, 'and so I favour local designers.'

Naomi could see why.

The fabrics were stunning, the lines exquisite and Naomi found herself trying on dresses that she never usually would.

'Try this one,' Jamal suggested. It was in a grey silver and long, and should have been completely over the top, but with the delicate henna flowers on her feet and with her hair down it somehow worked.

'I'm not sure,' Naomi said. Oh, she loved it but it wasn't anything like she usually wore.

'It's perfect on you. Let me get it for you,' Jamal said.

'Jamal.' Naomi shook her head. 'Please, don't offer. I find it awkward.'

'Of course.' Jamal nodded.

'I just want to like what I like.'

Jamal smiled and gave another nod. 'It's very beautiful, though.'

It was, and, the lines having been drawn, Naomi made one purchase to Jamal's ten.

'I've no idea when I'll ever wear it.'

'Tomorrow,' Jamal said. 'Allem and I want you both to come for dinner. You can wear it then.'

'For dinner?' Naomi laughed because this dress seemed over the top for dinner with friends but then realised that Jamal was completely serious.

'We want to say goodbye properly; it is so nice to have Sevastyan here. We want him to come to our home so dress up, Naomi. I shall.'

They had their hair done and really it was just a lovely day and topped off by high tea, where Naomi ate date-infused scones topped with rosewater jam. It was the holiday she had never really had.

No, it wasn't just that she was with Sev, but the amazing city, the wonderful company and taking the time to do fun things.

She even bought camel chocolates for her sisters and mailed them there and then.

Yes, she understood what Sev had said and why he had chosen to pull away from his family; she just wouldn't be pulling away from Kennedy and her other little sisters.

She imagined the two older girls' excitement when they opened their little parcels and, Naomi decided, staying around for them, even if from far away, felt like the right choice to have made.

Given Jamal and Allem's news, they found themselves in several baby boutiques and it was fun to see Jamal so excited.

'We had two years of trying,' Jamal said. 'I was starting to really worry and Allem was so good to me, he said it was me he wanted.'

'He's a very nice man.'

'He's so kind,' Jamal said. 'So romantic. Is Sev?'

Naomi just laughed. 'That would be a no.'

When surely they should have been finished, there was one thing more to do. 'I want look at rugs,' Jamal said. 'We will wait till we know what we are having before we choose but I'd love your thoughts.'

'I always wanted a Persian rug...' Naomi admitted, looking around.

'Not these,' Jamal said. 'We want to look only at the handmade.'

Oh, this baby would have everything!

They were exquisite and so expensive but, really, Naomi thought, when would she ever get a chance like this again? She was here in Dubai, shopping with an expert, because Jamal certainly knew her rugs.

'That's beautiful,' Jamal said, when she saw Naomi running her hand over one. The colours were amazing—a pistachio green, cream and black. Jamal parted the rug and checked the knots to see that it really was handmade but, really, it was so intricate and lavish that you couldn't doubt that it was.

It cost way more than Naomi could justify but it was far more beautiful than her conscience had allowed for and Jamal could see that she was wavering. 'Do you want me to bargain for you?' Jamal said. 'It will be half that price.'

'No.' Naomi shook her head. It was ridiculous but she could feel her eyes starting to sting so she quickly turned so that Jamal couldn't see. 'No, thanks. Come on...'

It was a tiny moment in a wonderful day and yet it stayed with her long after it had passed.

Naomi got back to the hotel, had a light dinner and then lay on the bed, trying to work out how she felt.

'God, it took for ever,' Sev said when he came in.

'Are you finished?'

'I have to go in at lunchtime and speak with the head of IT. Allem was right to get me in. How was your day with Jamal?'

'It was great.'

She went to get off the bed but he stopped her. 'Stay there, we've got to be up early tomorrow. We're going on a hot air balloon ride,' Sev said, as he started to undress. 'We've got to be there at five so we'll have to be up at four.'

'A hot air balloon ride?'

'It's supposed to be amazing. You go over the desert, you can see gazelles and…' Sev shrugged. He was suddenly far more interested in devouring her body.

It would have been a crime not to respond. Sev was as beautiful as the first time she'd seen him and the sex that night was as good as ever.

She had held on to a part of herself, though.

From day one in his bed she had.

Her heart might be in the ring but she'd never let him know that.

And afterwards, Naomi actually wished that they did have separate rooms. Her mind was too busy and there was no chance of falling asleep. She lay staring into the darkness as Sev slept and imagined the rug rolled up in her mother's spare room till she found somewhere to live.

How could you buy a rug when you didn't know where you were going to be living?

Then she pictured it by the fire on the floor of her apartment that she'd just let go in New York and it would have looked amazing.

And then she did a really stupid thing and imagined it on the floor in Sev's bedroom.

Its preferred home.

It went with the drapes, Naomi realised as she pictured it in her mind.

How long could she pretend that she wasn't in love with the man who lay next to her?

Naomi lay there, hit by a wave of homesickness so violent she could have packed her case right now—there was a need to go home.

She just didn't know where that was.

CHAPTER THIRTEEN

SEV WOKE TO his alarm and tried not to think of the date. So he lay there in the darkness, trying to motivate himself to get out of bed.

'Naomi?'

She woke to the sound of Sev saying her name and it was just as beautiful as the first time she had heard it. His hand was stroking her breast and he was tucked into her back. 'We have to get up.'

They did.

Bloody Allem and his ideas, Sev thought. He didn't want to go up in a balloon and be happy today.

Not today.

Or tomorrow.

These were the days he dreaded all year in their lead up.

Nikolai's last day.

He did not want to think about it.

'Sev—' Naomi started, but he interrupted her.

'Come on,' he said. 'If we want to get there in time.'

'Can I tell you something?'

He was right up behind her and she had never felt more comfortable in her life, warm, turned on. Tomorrow they would be up at the crack of dawn to get on the flight to London and she wanted to stay here and linger this morning.

'Tell me,' he said, but Naomi lost her train of thought as his hand lifted her hair and he kissed the back of her neck as he had wanted to do the night when he had played with her zipper.

His hand moved down from her breast to her stomach.

'Remember when I thought you were pregnant?'

Naomi smiled in the dark. 'I do.' Sev completely confused her—he'd turned down Emmanuel because he didn't speak Mandarin and Dianne for a nervous smile yet he'd offered her day care for her baby and to cut back on travel!

He was hard and she wished the little circular movement his hand made low on her stomach would never end, Naomi thought, even if she wanted his hand to move lower. So heavy was her arousal that she didn't want him to roll away and put on a condom, and her bottom pressed back into him. 'I'm on the Pill, Sev.'

'Thank God for that.'

He slid in unsheathed and let out a long sigh as the slippery warmth gripped him and they both ignored the sound of the snooze alarm.

'Sev…' 'They were both on the delicious edge. On the edge of desire, on the edge of coming, on the edge of over.

'Come on, baby.' He was moving faster and deeper, bringing her to the rapid high that he easily procured.

And so she told him something that she'd been trying to say since he'd come back last night—a simple truth.

Not *the* simple truth—after all she had promised no declarations—but she voiced another one. 'I don't want to go on the balloon ride.'

Naomi was starting to come, which he'd been pushing her to do. As her deep orgasm gripped him tight it drew Sev not just deeper into her but further away from thought.

Now the pre-dawn sky was a rich navy and a quickie was no longer enough. Sev didn't want to come down and face the day he dreaded, or go up in the air. He would rather be lost in the two of them.

And Naomi waited—for the delicious trip of him, for the intense pleasure to be topped. And it was, only not in the way she had anticipated.

He pulled out and Naomi thought, *What?*
What?
Then he turned her over.

'Sev?'

The alarm went again and he turned it off, and Naomi tried to get her breath as he faced her.

'We're not going up in a balloon.'

They stayed down on delicious earth.

He kissed her in a way he perhaps shouldn't if Naomi was going to keep her head.

Side on, eyes open for long enough to know what they were doing was breaking their rules.

Their legs were entwined, his cock nudged at her stomach, but now there was time for more. And so Naomi kissed him in a way perhaps she shouldn't. Three months of restraint had ended on the plane, but a different restraint ended this morning. She had never known a kiss like it. Their tongues swirled, mouths played with mouths. She took in his lower lip just to feel it between hers, they stroked at each other's mouths, caressed the other's tongue. Yes, she had never known a kiss like it and, she guessed, after this morning she never again would.

Naomi tasted love for the first time and she gave it back. She kissed him deep and slow, then his face, ear and down his neck. She breathed in the scent of him and savoured the taste of his skin on her tongue and lips as his hands roamed her body and read her like Braille.

He played with her breasts and then tasted them, lowering his head and his body too, so that his erection was on her thighs and they were rocking against each other as her hands went into his hair.

He took her nipple deep in his mouth and it felt like too much but not enough and then, in one motion, he lifted his head and found her mouth as his body came and fully joined hers.

Side on again, eyes open again, she looked right at him as he took her deep and slow.

If it was possible to be comfortable in scalding skin then she was. They were barely moving, face-to-face, with limbs entwined, both wanting the other's mouth but preferring eye contact.

They moved as one, changing tempo without thought, glad of sunrise just because they could take in the other's features.

Then they kissed, until each of Sev's thrusts became all-pervading, spreading through her body and then concentrating at her centre. He watched her lip turn down but not from tears. Sev felt her not just around his cock but it was as if her whole body tightened and they said nothing.

Yet.

Neither dared.

He released and she took and then took some more.

'Krasavitsa...'

She didn't want to know what it meant but he told her.

'Beautiful woman.'

She couldn't know he'd never said it to another.

CHAPTER FOURTEEN

FOUR THOUSAND FEET in the air would have been far safer.

Morning had more than broken, it was nearly midday when they woke up to Sev's phone and Ahmed, the IT guy, asking where he was.

Sev couldn't, Naomi noted, even look at her.

That was okay; she couldn't really look at him.

'I'm not sure how long I'll be,' Sev said.

'That's fine,' Naomi said.

Take your time! she thought.

Oh, there had been no declarations and after he had gone Naomi lay there, trying to convince herself that what had happened this morning had been no different from other times.

Liar.

And it wasn't just she who had broken the stated rules.

Sev had made love to her that morning and she knew, from the tension that now existed between them, that both of them regretted it.

For whatever reason he didn't want to get too involved or too close.

She did.

Worst of all, he'd let her glimpse what it could be like.

Sev went through all the changes with the head of IT but all day he found himself glancing at the time and thinking.

He remembered finishing school and taking the bus back to the orphanage with Nikolai.

He had been quiet.

That had suited him fine as he'd liked to do his homework on the bus and then read or study at night.

And then dinner.

Sixteen years ago they had lined up with their plates.

Now it was their last night in Dubai and it was to be spent being wined and dined by Allem.

'I'd rather it was just us tonight,' Sev admitted, as he dressed in his suit.

'And me,' Naomi admitted, but then she changed her mind. If it was just the two of them she might push for deeper conversation and demand answers about them.

Maybe there *was* safety in numbers.

'I'll call and tell him.'

'Sev!' Naomi halted him. 'No.'

'You just said you'd rather it was just us.'

'What we say and what we do are different things. He's gone out of his way to ensure that we have a good time. You can't just cancel on him.'

Oh, but he wanted to.

For more reasons than Naomi knew.

She put on her gorgeous silver dress and flat sandals and as Sev helped her with the zip there were no games this time.

'Come on, then,' Sev said.

No *You look nice*, or *Wow, I love that dress*.

And Naomi felt a burn of anger start to build.

She felt like emailing Emmanuel and asking him to order two dozen white roses.

It was that time, with Sev, she knew.

That time when the gloss had worn off and his interest waned.

She knew little of him but his routines she knew well.

'Naomi!' Jamal greeted her warmly and so too did Allem, but though the greeting was effusive and the dinner was magnificent there was tension in the air that Naomi couldn't read.

Sev wasn't at his most sociable but Naomi now knew Allem and Jamal accepted that.

There was something going on that she was not privy to, Naomi was sure.

'I had the chef make your favourite dessert, Sev,' Jamal said.

It was *sahlab*, a thick creamy milk pudding flavoured with orange blossom and rosewater. Topped with pistachios, it was delicious and light and Sev did comment.

'It's very nice.'

But then he glanced at his phone and, had the table been high enough to do so unseen, Naomi could cheerfully have kicked him.

Coffee was served and the shisha pipe came out. 'Would you like to see the nursery, Naomi?' Jamal asked.

Naomi smiled and nodded and as the women excused themselves Naomi thought back to their night in the desert and how light and easy life had seemed.

It was very different now.

Even Jamal seemed a touch strained, though she didn't comment or share her thoughts with Naomi.

Allem did with Sev.

Just as soon as the women were safely out of earshot, he turned to his friend.

'She said no?' Allem checked.

'I didn't ask her,' Sev admitted. 'Look, she's got some guy in England, maybe when she sees him…'

'Come off it, Sev.'

'I think he might be the safer bet.'

'You are being ridiculous.'

'No.' Sev shook his head. That morning had shaken him, that level of being with another person, feeling so close to another person, was one he wasn't sure he ever wanted to repeat.

'You didn't go up in the balloon?' Allem frowned.

'Nope,' Sev said, and tried not to think of what had happened. Instead he quickly changed the subject. 'I've spoken to Ahmed and I've told him I'll be back later next week. He seems to have a good grasp of the changes—'

'Sev, I don't want to talk about work tonight. Yesterday—'

'Was yesterday,' Sev interrupted. 'I've been thinking about things and while it's been a great break and we've both had a nice time…' They stopped talking as Jamal and Naomi came down the stairs.

'I'm sure Sev can rig up a system for you,' Naomi was saying.

'What was that?' Sev checked.

'Jamal is worried that the nursery and nanny's wing is too far from where they sleep.'

'I want to know if the baby cries,' Jamal said. 'I don't want to leave everything to the nanny.'

'Oh, please,' Allem said. 'We have the best security; we have monitors and cameras and, yes, of course we'll hear if the baby cries.'

About now, Sev thought.

About 11:00 p.m., sixteen years ago, the most important person in his world had cried.

And he'd heard him.

And then had rolled over and fallen back to sleep.

He thought of Nikolai.

No. Whatever he might have felt yesterday had long since passed. Sev did not trust himself to be the caretaker of another heart.

CHAPTER FIFTEEN

THEY'D STAYED ONE day and one night too long, Naomi thought as both her and Sev's alarms went off.

Three days and nights would have been enough and they could have ended it well.

She could have walked away having given them a chance but with her dignity intact.

Now she was doing her best not to cry.

Sev was right. Had she not messed up the schedule they'd be in London now and would already have parted ways.

Instead they lay in bed, barely touching and hardly talking.

Sev was thinking.

He had listened to Allem.

And he knew he couldn't ask her to come back to New York on a whim.

He'd bought a ring, yet he didn't know how to give it to her.

He scanned through his mind for even one example of a half-decent relationship that had survived the test of time.

Nyet.

Maybe Allem, but that was mainly business.

Anyway, he didn't have the space in his head for romance and maybes today. Instead he remembered what was.

Waking at five.

An hour earlier than usual but he and Nikolai had been on kitchen duty.

Sev had seen that the bed next to him had been empty.

Straight away he'd felt dread.

The first thing they'd usually done had been to make their beds.

It had been the very first thing that they'd done every morning without exception and yet Nikolai's bed had been unmade.

'We need to go,' Sev said, but he didn't need to. Naomi was already climbing out of bed.

She had packed yesterday.

For both of them.

Oh, as much as she might have pretended to herself that this was a holiday she was still on his payroll…for a few more hours at least. They drove to the airport and Naomi realised that this was finally it.

They boarded his jet and sat in silence.

Neither dared suggest bed.

Parting was already going to be hard enough.

'Where's your book?' Naomi asked, for something to say and because he always read during take-off.

Sev didn't answer her.

It was time to be practical. 'If I write up a reference,' Naomi asked, 'will you sign it?'

'I'll do one for you now.'

He took out his computer.

'How long did you work for me?' Sev checked.

'Three months.' Naomi sighed. He didn't even know that.

'I meant, how long do you want me to put that you have worked for me?'

'Just put the truth,' Naomi snapped.

Sev actually smiled. She was the only person he knew who growled as they asked you to write a reference for them.

'Testy?' Sev checked.

'Tired,' Naomi corrected.

Sev typed for a couple of moments and then flicked the result over to her computer. 'Let me know if you want me to change anything.'

Naomi opened the file and read it.

To Whom It May Concern,

Naomi Johnson has worked as my personal assistant for three very long months.

Initially when I interviewed her I decided she wasn't suitable for the role—she said 'sorry' a lot and that irritated me—but then I decided to give her a try.

I have regretted that choice at times.

Naomi Johnson was moody, didn't like ordering flowers and she was, I have to say, obstructive on occasion. Now, though, I understand that her belligerent attitude was because she wanted to have sex with me.

And I did with her.

I wish we hadn't waited so long but I'm also glad that we did.

In summary, Naomi Johnson is the best PA I've ever had, the nicest person I've known, and I feel a bit sick typing this because, though I don't want her to leave, I honestly think it's for the best that she does.

Sevastyan Derzhavin

PS I shall write you a real one now.

Naomi read it without comment and, as nice as it was, it made her feel cross too. For all they had found, he would let her leave, and while she might know him better, she understood him less.

It was a long, lonely flight.

Sev did write her a real reference.

One that was so good it had Naomi question if she should go back to her old job.

This could open doors.

She wanted to be walking through his, though.

The hardest thing ever, far harder than leaving her father behind, was to walk off the plane and to his car. She had sworn she wouldn't break down in front of him and that was a promise to herself that was getting more difficult to keep by the minute.

'I think my mother may have come to meet me,' Naomi said. 'Can your car drop me off at Arrivals?'

Sev didn't like that idea. He had thought he would be taking her home but instead his driver took them the relatively short distance to Arrivals.

'Leave your bags,' Sev said. 'Go and find your mother and then I can take you both home.'

'There's no need,' Naomi said. 'We can make our own way home.'

'No, my driver—'

'My mother has a car,' Naomi interrupted. 'We're hardly going to travel in separate vehicles.'

So this was it.

They stood as a trolley was loaded with her things, shivering in the damp morning air, and though Sev knew he was doing the right thing by her—that she would be far better off without him—it was harder than it had ever been to say goodbye to another person.

Usually his PAs left and, as long as he had another in place, he had given it little thought.

It was the same with lovers.

There was always another.

Family.

Ah, don't go there.

Friends.

Sev watched as the last bag was loaded onto the trolley.

Friends were the reason he was here in London, no doubt to sit waiting and to be let down all over again.

She turned and looked at Sev, the most beautiful man in the world, who had made love to her like he adored her. A man who had taken her heart and pocketed it like a piece of loose change.

'Thanks for everything, Sev.' She was able to look him in the eye. 'If Emmanuel needs any information—'

'I'll call you if there are any issues,' Sev interrupted.

'Please, don't,' Naomi responded. She didn't want to hear that voice pulling her back under his spell again. 'Emmanuel can email me. Anyway...' she took out her phone from her pocket '...this is yours.'

He had switched her over to a work phone on the day that she had started.

'Keep it,' Sev said, because it was far more than a work phone that she was handing back, it was a safety net should he change his mind, a line of communication she was severing.

'I don't need it,' Naomi said.

She didn't.

The very last thing she needed as she moved on with the next stage of her life was a phone that might ring, a text that might bleep. Oh, her heart would soar, Naomi knew, and it would no doubt be him, asking where some file was, or had she responded to…?

Or…

She looked into his eyes and she had no doubt, no doubt at all, that he might be cruel enough to call her deep into a long night, to toy with her heart just because he was bored.

'Here.' When he didn't take it she popped it into his top suit pocket and he just stood there.

'I've got your private number,' Sev warned.

'I'm changing it,' Naomi said.

It was the very first thing she would do.

And she would only open emails that came from Emmanuel.

Screw you for letting me leave, she wanted to shout, but didn't.

'What will you do?' Sev asked.

'Do?' Naomi frowned. 'I'll get back to the real world.'

One without castles in the sky.

One without a morning being made love to at sunrise followed by a cold grey goodbye.

He went into his coat and pulled out a slim package and handed it to her. 'Your leaving present.'

He just hurt her again and again.

Naomi didn't want a leaving present; she wanted him.

'I'm going to miss you,' Sev said.

'Not that much,' Naomi replied.

After all, he was letting her leave.

Her trolley was one of those that moved to the left and Naomi steered it badly, wishing that the automatic door would open more quickly, instead of leaving her standing a few seconds too long.

A terrible few seconds because she did turn around, just in time to see his car sliding off.

No lingering stare, nothing.

Sev had got back into his car and got on with his life.

Now it was time for her to do the same.

CHAPTER SIXTEEN

HE WOULD MISS her *that* much.

So much that, even if today could never be an easy one, it could be less unbearable.

'Pull in here,' Sev said to his driver.

He was trying to dissuade himself from going after her. The kindest thing would surely be to let her get back to her life, rather than hazard her with his first adult attempt at a relationship.

His phone buzzed and, rather than get out of the car, he checked it.

And then hope came back to his heart.

There was his niece, Mariya, smiling into the camera and showing off the pink earrings that he had bought for her eighteenth birthday. There was message beneath.

I told Ma that the earrings were from Zena, my friend at school. She thinks they are cheap and so I can keep them. Thank you Uncle Sevastyan.
I love them very much.
I love you too.
Mariya

The words were followed by two pink hearts, and for all that was wrong in the world there was still something right.

Every year he had sent his niece a gift but this year he had sent two.

One to her home.

The other, the earrings, to her school.

He cared not if they had been lost.

He cared a lot more that they had been found.

If he could just get through today… Sev thought.

If he could explain to Naomi the disappointment of Daniil not showing up and the black memories of this day…

Sev doubted he could, not today.

But something inside him doubted she would mind.

Was that love?

Where you wait with patience, where you hold on till the other is ready?

Maybe it was time to find out.

Arrivals at Heathrow was hell. It was all families and happy couples and tender reunions. Had she had her phone on her then Naomi would have texted her mother to see if she was here and ask her to meet her outside. But Naomi's old phone was in her case.

So she stood, scanning the crowd, deciding that her mother hadn't got her message, or, if she had, that she'd decided not to come.

Yes, it was a lonely morning and as she turned to head off, tears in her eyes, Naomi hit a solid wall, one her heart recognised because the tears she had held back started to fall as she was held in his arms.

'Too much,' Sev said. 'I will miss you too much if I let you go back now.'

He kissed her and she hated herself for kissing him back. It was a sizzling, passionate kiss, one where he moved her from the crowds and Naomi found herself pressed to a wall and she could almost taste the blood from the bruise of Sev's mouth.

He offered her nothing, an extension perhaps, and she loathed herself that she would take his crumbs.

But she would.

And she loathed herself that on a freezing morning he pulled her into his coat and he was hot and hard for her, and for all the pain of goodbyes to come she still wanted him.

He wanted away from the crowds, he wanted sex and then maybe to talk. And she wanted him—that trip in her that he recognised on sight, that shift where her body turned over to him was there.

'Airport hotel?' Sev asked.

'You are *such* a bastard!' She laughed, she cried, she was about to say yes.

'What the…?' Sev started, but he never got to finish. Instead he was literally hauled out of her arms and swung around.

All Naomi said was a flash of red and then a fist and then the sight of Sev flying back against the wall where she stood, but like being against the ropes in a boxing ring he propelled himself outwards.

'No one else?' a man shouted, and her mind was still spinning from the kiss and its rude interruption, but then she saw who it was.

'Andrew?' Naomi looked up and saw red foil heart balloons floating up to the roof and realised he must have come to meet her.

And so too did Sev.

He had come out fighting and, given the life he had led, that he would floor this guy was a foregone conclusion.

But then he heard who it was.

The next fist to his gut he took.

But then, when Naomi tried to come between them, shouting to Andrew that he had no right and Andrew responded with words Naomi did not deserve, Sev saw red—only they weren't heart-shaped balloons.

Sev went to floor him but four strong arms were holding him back—Security had arrived and, looking around at the stunned travellers, Sev tried to keep his breathing even, telling himself to calm down, that an airport, and being sober at that, was no place to fight. He was also telling himself that had Naomi been his fiancée, he'd have been just as furious as this guy was.

'I'm fine,' Sev said to Security.

'You're sure about that?' one responded.

'Sure.'

'Because—' It was the security guard who didn't get to finish their sentence this time because, unlike Sev, Andrew was unrestrained and still angry as he took his cowardly chance.

Naomi let out a scream as Sev's head was violently hit and knocked backwards.

The security moved quickly to restrain Andrew, leaving Sev to fall to the floor, and her quiet homecoming disappeared in a blur of police and then paramedics.

'No need…' Sev slurred, when they insisted on taking him to the hospital.

'There is, Sev,' Naomi said. 'You were knocked out.'

'For how long?' one of the paramedics asked.

'Three minutes.'

They had been the longest three minutes of Naomi's life.

She hadn't looked up, she hadn't cared that Andrew was being arrested—all she'd been able to think of was Sev.

Which wasn't a first—for the past four months almost all she had been able to think of was him.

Who was she kidding? Naomi thought as she got into the ambulance he had been stretchered into and the doors were closed.

As if a brave goodbye could change anything.

Her heart belonged to him.

Even if she was terrified and terribly worried it became apparent, about ten seconds into their arrival, that Sev, though terribly vital to her, was rather way down on the list of priorities.

The triage nurse checked him and Naomi wished she had a little triage desk in her heart.

She did have one.

On the day they had met it had spoken to her and strongly suggested that this man was trouble, that if she let him in, even a little way, she'd surely regret it.

Only she didn't.

'What the hell is this place?' Sev asked an hour or so later, when he was dressed in a gown and had come to better but was still groggy and growing increasingly irritable, which the nurse said wasn't a good sign.

He'd been irritable for a few days, Naomi wanted to point out.

'Why didn't you get them to take me somewhere private?' Sev demanded.

'The paramedics don't care if you're a billionaire,' Naomi said. 'They took you to the nearest hospital.'

'And now we'll be here for the next fortnight, waiting to be seen. I don't need hospital.'

'You need to be stitched.'

There was a huge gash over his left eye and it had closed over. He kept going to sleep, only to wake up angrier every time he woke up and demanding to know the time.

'It's eleven a.m.,' the nurse said. 'You're just waiting to go around for an MRI.'

'I don't need an MRI.'

'You're drowsy.'

'Because I haven't slept since…' Sev looked up at the peeling ceiling and he recognised it well, or rather he recognised that type of ceiling and he remembered Nikolai and that he had to meet Daniil.

'Where's my phone?'

'Here,' Naomi said. She had picked it up when he'd dropped it in the fight but as she handed it over it turned on and Naomi let out a shocked gasp.

There were the earrings he had bought from Tiffany's but the girl who was wearing them was in school uniform.

'Hell, Sev,' Naomi shouted. 'When you said she was young…!'

'It's my niece, Mariya,' Sev said. 'I got them for her eighteenth birthday.'

'Oh.'

And Naomi sat back on the plastic seat, as Sev lay squinting into his phone.

'Last year I sent a necklace and it was sold online by Renata. I don't know if Mariya even saw the necklace so I sent these to her school.'

Naomi sat there, thinking. It was a very smart uniform that Mariya was wearing.

Private-school smart.

And, no, she could live for a hundred years and not fully know him.

Yet she was starting to work him out.

'You sent that money, didn't you.'

'Sorry?'

'The money for Mariya's treatment.'

'Of course I did.'

'Why?' Naomi asked. 'Why would you do that when knew you were being scammed?'

'As I told Renata, she would have had the money anyway. I always wanted my niece to have a good education and for my sister to have nice things.'

Then he corrected himself.

'Half-sister. She has the money but we don't talk any more.'

Now Sev's body demanded sleep again but there was somewhere he needed to be.

'Naomi, I need to get to Buckingham Palace...'

'It will still be there tomorrow,' the nurse said as she checked his blood pressure.

'But I have to be there at midday.'

Naomi was starting to seriously worry about his head injury now—there was no place that Sev ever *needed* to be. This was a man who could arrive eight hours late for a meeting with a sheikh without making so much as an apology.

He never got upset or agitated and yet he clearly was now.

'Sev, you have to have this scan.'

'I don't have to do anything, apart from get there.'

''What's so important that it can't wait?'

'It doesn't matter.'

Sev lay there and decided that as soon as the nurse and Naomi left he would disappear.

'Can you go and get me a drink?' He turned to Naomi.

'We're keeping you nil by mouth for now,' the cheerful nurse said, and then left them.

'I'm sorry,' Naomi said, and he gritted his teeth as she went to apologise for her ex-fiancé.

'Don't start apologising,' Sev said. 'I thought I'd got that far with you at least. It isn't your fault if your fiancé—'

'My ex.'

'What?'

'I dumped him.'

'Er…when?'

'The night before I resigned.'

'And you didn't think to tell me? I let him hit me…'

'I know you did.'

And then he put Andrew in the file he had first assigned him to—irrelevant.

'I need to be somewhere, Naomi.'

'You can't leave yet.'

He bloody well could. Sev sat up and Naomi decided there was nothing sadder than seeing someone so strong and determined rendered incapable.

He squinted at the drip and that clever brain was foggy as he tried to work out how to get it down, and then he looked at the curtain that separated them from the world.

'Where's my wallet?'

'In the safe.' The cheery nurse was back. 'So I suggest you lie there.'

She had never seen such defeat on someone's face.

And then she watched as he came up with a solution and those grey eyes turned to her.

'Can you go there for me?'

'To Buckingham Palace?' Naomi frowned. 'Sev, I think you might be a bit confused.'

'I've never been less confused,' Sev said. 'I go there each year and I cannot miss being there.'

'Why?'

'In case Daniil shows up. I wrote to him a few years ago and asked him to meet me at midday on November the twelfth and he never showed.'

'You think he might now?'

'No,' Sev admitted. 'I just don't want to miss out on the slim chance he might.'

'Okay,' Naomi said. 'What does he look like?'

'I haven't seen him since he was twelve. Black hair, tall...'

It wasn't an awful lot to go on.

'He's Russian,' Sev added.

'I'd worked that one out.' Naomi said. She could feel herself being dragged back into the vortex. A couple of hours ago he had been willing to take her to the airport hotel, Naomi reminded herself.

She deserved more than that.

'I'll do this, Sev, and then I'll come back and let you know what happened, but then I'm going home.'

And so she sat in the rain by the fountain and watched the world go by.

She was so angry with Andrew, so angry with Sev too, for prolonging the agony.

They should be over with by now.

She should be unpacking her case, instead of sitting on the ledge of a cold stone statue.

It was hopeless.

There were a few tourists, all huddled under their umbrellas, and some people walking around. How the hell was she supposed to pick out a man with black hair from the hundred or so other men with black hair? She saw a blonde woman smiling brightly, clapping her hands, and she had that sort of determined look that the rain didn't matter and that she was here for the duration.

So too, it would seem, was Naomi.

It was after one when she finally gave in.

There was no one—no one at all.

She gave a thin smile to the blonde woman, who was looking around too, and then Naomi watched as she went over to a man.

A moody-looking resigned man who shrugged and started to walk off, but the woman argued with him, pulled at his coat.

And, yes, he was tall and had black hair and so Naomi made her way over.

'Daniil?'

She could look the biggest fool ever here, Naomi knew. 'Daniil?'

'I told you!' The blonde woman exclaimed. 'Sevastyan?'

'Well, if it is, then you've got a lot better looking,' Daniil said. Naomi started to laugh as they were all so stunned and sort of staring at each other, not really knowing what to do.

'I'm Sev's PA. He wanted to be here—'

'I am here.'

Naomi turned and there was Sev, as white as putty but stitched, and she watched as the two men shook hands.

No, it wasn't a tender reunion. Maybe Sev just didn't go for that type of thing.

They spoke in Russian with guarded voices and Naomi looked at the other woman.

'I'm Libby.' She smiled, rubbing her hands together from the cold.

Naomi saw her rings. 'You're Daniil's wife?'

'Yes!' Libby nodded. 'It feels strange, saying that. We just got married yesterday.'

'Congratulations,' Naomi offered, and then she looked back at the two men and she would never understand Sev because he concluded the conversation and walked back over to them.

'It's good to meet you, Libby,' he said. 'Congratulations on your marriage.'

'Thank you.'

'It's good to be back in touch with Daniil but right now you two need to get on with your honeymoon and I need to get to the hotel.' He looked at Naomi. 'Come on, we ought to go.'

He shook hands again with Daniil.

Was that it?' Naomi pondered as Daniil and Libby walked off. All those years together and then all those years apart and yet they'd chatted for all of ten minutes.

That was who Sev was, though, Naomi realised, cold and dismissive.

It was she who had refused to accept that.

'You have to watch me,' Sev said, and handed her a head-injury leaflet. 'They wanted to keep me in and only let me go on the proviso that I'm checked every hour until morning.'

'Get a nurse, then.'

'No, I don't want some stranger watching me sleep. If I did, I'd have stayed in the hospital.'

'Well, tough, I don't work for you any more.'

'Fine.' He hailed a cab and climbed in.

And he would, he bloody well would, Naomi thought, he'd just go and sleep alone.

'One night,' Naomi said, getting into the taxi. Looking at his grey complexion, Sev wasn't asking her there to seduce her.

That much she knew.

Naomi dealt with check-in and when they got to his suite Sev didn't even fully undress, he just kicked off his shoes and socks and then went to deposit his hospital bag with his wallet and things in the safe.

'What's my code?' Sev asked.

'I'll do it,' Naomi said.

'I can manage,' Sev said, and punched in the numbers. Once done, he went and lay on the bed and Naomi closed the drapes and just sat.

'How was he?' she asked. 'Your friend?'

Sev shrugged.

'He asked me what had happened with Roman,' Sev said. 'I told him that I don't know anything. I got a scholarship at fifteen and left then.'

'What about the other one, Nikolai?' Naomi asked. 'Did he know?'

'What? That he had died?' Sev easily said what she had struggled to voice. 'Daniil had already found that out—apparently he was being abused.' There was no emotion Sev's voice, just the exhaustion of a very cruel life. 'I didn't know that.'

'I'm sorry.'

'I let him down,' Sev admitted. 'He was crying one night and I didn't know if he'd want me to say anything. The dormitory was not very private at the best of times. So I let it go, pretended I hadn't noticed. Then he cried again and I asked him what was wrong. And he told me to leave it. I did. The next day he'd run away. They found him a week later, and his bag with this ship he'd made by the river.'

'The one on your desk at home?'

'Yep. It's not much to show for a life,' Sev said, slowly drifting off into an exhausted sleep.

Naomi woke him every hour, just enough to be sure that he was okay, but by 7:00 p.m. she was exhausted too and she watched as he woke up.

Sev tried to guess the time.

Then the month and year.

And then he tried to work out their location.

'You're in London.' Naomi said.

'So I am.'

And he remembered again that before such a violent interruption they had been heading to the airport hotel…

'Come to bed.'

'No, thank you.' Naomi said. 'I'm supposed to watch you till morning, according to the leaflet, and then I'm going to go.'

'Where?'

'Home,' Naomi said. 'Well, to my mum's for a couple of weeks and then I'll find somewhere…'

Somewhere.

It was a horrible word at times.

Somewhere to get over you.

'My head hurts,' Sev said.

'You're due for some painkillers.'

'Not that head.'

She didn't want to laugh but that was the problem— he could turn her smile on even when her heart was in shreds.

'Come to bed,' Sev said. 'God, the day I've had, I need a shag.'

'Well, seeing as you put it so nicely.'

He had the nerve to ignore her sarcastic response and pulled the covers back.

'Not a chance.' Naomi turned and looked at him and his lazy heart that had let her leave. 'If Andrew hadn't hit you, we'd be over with now.'

'Wind back,' Sev said, as if she was some bloody computer. 'I'd suggested that we go to the airport hotel.'

'You're *so* romantic.'

'No, I'm not.'

'I'm going to order dinner,' Naomi said. 'Do you want anything?'

He didn't.

As Naomi went into her bag to get the tip ready she saw her leaving present. She would wait till he was asleep to open it.

There was a knock on the door and in came her dinner.

'Good,' Sev said, and sat up. 'I'm starving.' And he saw her blow out an angry breath and then wheel the silver trolley over to him. 'I was joking,' Sev said. 'Enjoy your meal. I'll have a glass of champagne, though…'

'You can't drink with a head injury,' Naomi said. 'According to the leaflet.'

'That's not very nice of you.'

'I never said I'd be a nice nurse.'

She ate the most delicious steak ever, with truffle butter, and she drank champagne and watched his wry smile as he heard her top up her glass.

'You are a cruel tease.'

'I know,' Naomi said.

'Go into my jacket,' Sev said. 'Daniil gave me a copy of a picture.'

She went to his jacket and sat down to look at a photo of four young boys from a lifetime ago.

'Daniil's an identical twin.'

'Yep.'

How cruel, Naomi thought. It had been bad enough knowing that twins had been split up, but that they were identical made it seem somehow worse.

'He can't find Roman. From what Daniil has been able to find out, it would seem that he shacked up with Anya for a while after he left the orphanage and then left—'

'Anya?'

'The cook's daughter. Daniil said that she's a famous ballerina now.'

Naomi looked back at the picture and at Nikolai. Well, it had to be him because other boy was Sev.

'You were a nerd.'

'I was,' Sev said. 'I am.'

The sexiest nerd in the world, though.

CHAPTER SEVENTEEN

SEV FINALLY WENT to sleep and Naomi put the tray outside the door and then, when that didn't wake him, she took out her present and quietly opened it.

His book?

Why?

It was old and tattered and the one that he always read on take-off.

She'd made a joke once about what a slow reader he was. That had been in Mali and that had been when he'd put down the book and, er, suggested that she might need a little lie-down under him.

'Or on top.' Sev had grinned. 'I'm generous like that.'

It had been the most direct offer of sex she had ever had.

Hell, she'd been tempted but had told him off and Sev had got back to his book.

She opened it and frowned. It was all in Russian but as she turned the pages she saw some pictures, just black-and-white ones but it took just a few moments of looking to realise it was a book of fairy tales.

He'd read them to his friends, he had told her that.

She saw a photo of a wolf that had a woman draped over it and she looked at this beautiful, complex man, who was glib and dismissive and yet sat reading old fairy tales on take-off.

A man who said he didn't want relationships yet had spent five years standing outside a palace in the hope of finding a friend.

And she saw it then. Pain. Not the pain of his head injury, she was sure, just the agony of so many losses that were etched on his face.

And she understood a little more how hard today must have been. No, there could be no effusive greeting after so much hurt.

And she knew why the men had stood back from each other, how they'd had to stay distant to stay standing.

Who could blame him for 'needing a shag', as he'd so nicely put it today?

And who could blame her for wanting him?

Naomi put the book beside the bed, undressed and got in.

She was, Sev thought, like a pillow, but better than, and he rolled into her.

'You're a nice surprise,' Sev said, and ran a hand along her body and felt her naked. 'That's an even nicer surprise.'

He just breathed her in.

'Both heads hurt,' Sev said.

She hadn't expected a gymnastic event as they shared a kiss, a long slow one, but face-to-face sex was something she couldn't deal with again. Not the sort where you looked at each other and your eyes made promises that by daylight you could not keep.

So she went down on him but on the way she took in those Merlot-coloured nipples and that flat stomach that had always tempted her.

And so to her favourite part and she took her time because it must be the last time.

He stroked her as lazily as if he were stroking a cat and turned her on just as easily as he always did.

There was little noise, just the sounds they made and that moan he gave that signalled the end, and he spread his fingers inside her and stretched her as he came.

It hurt, but it was amazing to come to his palm as she swallowed him down, and then he pulled her up to lie with him.

'I'll return the favour tomorrow,' Sev said.

Favour?

He made her too angry to sleep at times.

A favour.

An itch.

That was all it was to him.

As Sev dozed she took down the book from the shelf and started not to read it, it was in Russian after all, but to turn the pages.

'Remember your interview when you said you'd read in bed?' Sev asked sleepily.

'Ha-ha…'

'What are you reading?'

'My present,' Naomi answered. 'Sev, why would you give this to me?'

'Because you still believe in them.'

'And you don't?'

'The dark bits,' Sev said. 'I don't know what I believe today. It's a bad day.'

'How can it be a bad day when you're back in touch with your friend?' Naomi asked.

'Because today is Nikolai's anniversary, or rather it is the day when we found out he was missing. Yes, I saw Daniil and one day, tomorrow maybe, we will be so glad to be in touch, but for today, I know, he misses his twin and that he wishes it could be me...'

'No.'

'Yes,' Sev said, 'because today I wished it was Nikolai that I stood and spoke with. To apologise, to go back...'

'To what?'

'He cried that night. I can't remember him crying before that, not once. I can't remember any of us crying. And when I heard him I just didn't know what to say. I didn't know if he'd be embarrassed. I thought we could talk on kitchen duty the next morning and then I couldn't ignore it and so I asked what was wrong and he said to leave it. I did. I left it be. The next morning he was gone. Naomi, I rolled over and I was all he had and yet I rolled over and went to sleep.'

'Like this?' Naomi said, and she closed her eyes.

'Don't joke,' he warned.

'Oh, I'm not joking. You just said you lay there thinking how embarrassed he might be that you could hear him, that you couldn't remember any of you crying...so were you thinking those things when you *let it be*? Or did you roll over and try to work out what the hell to do?'

'I was going to talk to him on kitchen duty. I should have handled it differently.'

'Who knows?' Naomi said. 'Maybe he wanted to just cry and not have the whole dormitory wake up. Were Daniil and Roman there?'

'No,' Sev said. 'Daniil had been adopted by then and Roman had been moved to another area. I told you,' Sev said, 'I'm crap at emotion.'

'Not really,' Naomi said. 'When I was upset on the plane you were very lovely to me. You told me stuff you didn't want to.' She thought for a moment. 'The night of my father's party, when I was upset, you came to see what was wrong.'

'And made things a whole lot worse between us.'

'Oh, I think that might have been me.' Naomi smiled.

They just lay there and it was Naomi who rolled over as she had never felt more tired.

'Go to sleep.'

'I'm supposed to check you every hour.'

'Go to sleep,' Sev said. 'I'll set the alarm.'

Yet he knew he didn't need to. If something happened she was there, half awake, half asleep, as he had been that night.

Naomi was right.

Sev had lain awake for hours, trying to think of how to best broach things with Nikolai the next day.

And, whether he'd handled that night badly, at the very least he had learned from it.

Sev would not leave her alone and crying.

He hadn't, in fact.

CHAPTER EIGHTEEN

'WHAT TIME IS IT?' Sev asked.

Naomi opened her eyes to the familiar question from him and glanced at the bedside clock.

'Six,' she said and then added, 'A.m.'

Just in case.

But she wasn't paid to be his speaking clock any more, and so she made herself do it.

Made herself sit up and get out of his bed.

She went and had a shower.

She didn't want him.

Oh, she loved him, she was crazy about him, but she didn't want him.

It was the biggest revelation of her life.

No longer did she want someone who so clearly didn't want her. Or, if he did, then he wanted her just a bit and she wasn't prepared for his crumbs. For sex when he felt like it, for conversation when it suited him.

It wasn't just Sev she was saying goodbye to but a lifetime spent waiting for the cavalry to arrive for her.

It just had.

It was her.

'What are you doing?' Sev asked, as she got dressed.

'I watched you last night.' Naomi said. 'That was what we agreed to.'

'You did a bit more than watch me,' Sev said. 'Do you sleep with all your patients, nurse?'

And she laughed.

He would always make her laugh, even with a broken heart.

'I am going,' Naomi said.

'Why would you leave when things are just getting interesting?'

'They got interesting for me a few months ago, Sev. I'm not waiting around for you to decide how much I mean to you, or if you might keep me around a while longer. I'm not tiptoeing around waiting for you to change your mind one day, or not.'

He had never been more proud of another person.

Never.

And, Sev knew, because he'd been thinking all night, that this he could now do.

November had always been his most hated month.

Her leaving would make it hell for ever.

'Could you get something from the safe?' Sev asked.

'Get it yourself.'

'I'm sick,' Sev said, and tapped his closed eye and the mess her ex-fiancé had made of his face. 'Do you think I'll scar?'

She picked up her case but he had pushed her guilt switch so Naomi did stop at the safe on the way out.

'You're not very good at your alphabet, are you?' he commented.

She was in no mood for his games.

'N is the fourteenth letter,' Sev said, just as she went to key in one, four.

And A was the first, Naomi knew as she typed in one.

'You're my secret code,' Sev said. 'You're the key that opens the door.'

'What are you doing, Sev?'

He had changed his code a few weeks ago…

'In Helsinki,' Sev answered her thoughts. 'I've been crazy about you since then.'

'Why didn't you tell me?'

'I tried,' Sev said. 'I told you then I was cured of blondes.'

'And so you took yourself off to Italy!' Naomi snarled.

She had been so jealous of Miss Roma but, then again, maybe that was more because she had thought the earrings were for her.

And then she had to smile.

'Mali,' Sev reminded her. 'I wanted you then.'

'You have the worst chat-up lines.'

'They usually work just fine.'

Yes, Naomi conceded, they probably worked just fine when it was only sex you wanted.

She wanted more.

"What's in the safe, Naomi?"

There was a black velvet pouch.

Real velvet, and she was nervous about opening it because she could not stand for hope to be dashed again.

She opened the pouch and into her palm fell the most exquisite piece of jewellery she had ever seen, but she quickly looked away.

'I bought this for you in Dubai. I was going to tell you to dump that loser and then I decided against it.'

'You regretted buying it…'

'We are so going to work on your self-confidence,' Sev warned. 'No, I felt I had no right to be moving on with my life near the anniversary of my friend's death. Neither was I sure I could make you happy. I'm very sure I can now.'

He always had.

Despite the heartbreak of loving him, Sev had always made her smile.

'Marry me.'

'Sev!' He didn't have to go that far!

'Naomi Derzhavin.'

'Sev, please don't joke.'

'I've never been more serious in my life,' Sev said. 'Come here.'

She walked over in her coat and sat on the edge of the bed.

'I want you to be my family,' Sev said. 'I want us to make each other happy and we do. I want my book by our bed…' She looked at the ring. 'I know I need to open up and I'll try.'

Naomi looked into the eyes of a man who didn't need to change,

Well, maybe a bit.

But he could be as depraved as he liked just as long as it was with her.

'It's a very rare, natural black diamond,' Sev said, and now she let herself look. In the intricate setting there were also white diamonds. 'The metal is platinum with rhodium plate,' Sev explained. 'I chose rhodium for its rarity and strength but it's not very malleable…' Naomi smothered a smile—he'd be taking her through the periodic table soon.

Sev looked at the ring.

There was no doubt as to its beauty.

No doubt as to its recipient.

His doubt had been in him.

Not now.

'Do you know why I chose black?' Sev said.

Of course Naomi did. 'Because it's my favourite colour.'

'At first,' he said, 'but there were a few to choose from and then I found out this stone's name—Unseen Star. You might be an unseen star for some but never by me.'

'You *are* romantic.'

'I'll try to be,' Sev said. 'But I'm a bastard too—I think we can both safely agree that this blows Andrew's ring out of the water.'

'It does.' Naomi smiled.

He put it on and, honestly, it was amazing.

She had never cared for jewellery much but any woman would love this ring.

Especially when given by him.

'It was supposed to go well with that silver dress that you had on the other night.'

And Naomi remembered Jamal insisting that it was perfect when Naomi hadn't been sure. 'Jamal and Allem knew?' She frowned. 'Even about the ring?'

'Naomi,' Sev said, 'I asked Allem for advice…'

He did love her.

She knew it for sure then.

'I listened to Allem but it wasn't me. I needed to do this myself and I needed to get certain dates out of the way before I got to be happy.'

They shared a lovely kiss.

Sev naked, she in her coat, but not for very long as he was already slipping it off. 'You can't say no to me. Jamal and Allem have already got us an engagement present.'

'Was that what was wrong with them the other night?' Oh, she understood now! 'I thought they were a bit off.'

'You were supposed to arrive wearing the ring! Allem had said I should take you up on a balloon and propose. Naomi, can you really see me coming up with that?' Sev asked. 'Me?'

'No!' She couldn't and she was actually glad of that. 'I didn't want to go up in a balloon either.'

'See how suited we are.'

'Do you want to know what our present is?' Sev asked. 'It's a rug. And, by amazing coincidence, when Allem sent me a photo of it, I saw that it goes with my curtains. How lucky is that?'

She was as red in the face as when first he'd met her but she was laughing now.

'You are tragic, Naomi.'

'I know!'

'One piece of housekeeping,' Sev said, before he slipped the ring on her finger. 'If you ever flirt with another man when you're wearing this, the way you flirted with me—'

'Er…Sev,' Naomi interrupted. 'If we look back over the last few months, I think my behaviour is the pale one and that was fake and this isn't. And,' she added, 'I didn't flirt with you.' She'd always been holding back. 'You haven't seen me flirting.'

'Yet,' Sev said.

He couldn't wait.

Finally November felt better.

The world felt better for both for them.

EPILOGUE

'YOU LOOK BEAUTIFUL, Naomi,' Anderson said.

She had her father's approval.

Naomi just didn't need it now.

For six months she had had Sev's love and that made her stronger and the world all a touch clearer.

Together they had decided on London for the wedding. That was her home and, even if she wasn't particularly close to her mother, Naomi had felt a New York wedding might seem a snub.

It also meant Daniil could be there as his wife, Libby, was heavily pregnant.

Sev and Daniil were in regular touch now and slowly the past was being uncovered, which was painful at times but something both men felt they had to do.

In the six months since their engagement, Anderson Anderson had courted Sev—taking him along to his golf club and proudly introducing his future son-in-law, and for her, Naomi knew, Sev had gone along with it.

Sev did things for her that she never could have expected. He made her happier than she had ever thought she could be and so, today she was doing something for him.

Something that was also for her.

Anderson had brought Judy and Naomi's little sisters

to London. Kennedy was her bridesmaid but the others were all there in the church. Now Naomi stood in a hotel room and she knew that her father, who had never hopped on a plane for her, was here only because of Sevastyan and the contacts that name would gather when dropped.

It was father-and-daughter time.

Kennedy was safely in the car with Naomi's other bridesmaid, a friend who, unlike her father, had been there since schooldays.

'We'll have another celebration when we get home,' Anderson said. 'Judy's family and our friends and colleagues—'

'No,' Naomi interrupted. 'I doubt there will be another celebration. If there is then it will be a quiet affair.' She took a breath and looked her father straight in the eye. 'And I won't tell you about it. I'll forget to invite you, just as you did to me on your fiftieth birthday party.'

Anderson had the decency at least to look uncomfortable.

'It was a surprise party,' he attempted.

'I don't think so.' Naomi shook her head. 'And even if it was supposed to be a surprise, why wouldn't Judy invite me? It wasn't as if she didn't have the opportunity— I was there that week, babysitting for you. Anyway, I thought it was your second wife who had an issue with me, or that was the excuse you gave.'

'Let's not do this on your wedding day,' Anderson suggested. 'I don't want you upsetting yourself.'

'I'm not upset, though,' Naomi said. 'I was then. I came to bring you a cake and you were having a party with the people who meant something to you.'

'Come on, Naomi. Not today.'

'Yes, today,' Naomi said. She stood in her wedding dress and was far from the blushing bride. 'You gave me away a long time ago,' Naomi said. 'There's no need for you to do it again today.'

'It will look—'

'Yes,' she interrupted, 'it will look a bit odd if you go to the church now and sit with your wife and my sisters, but that's what you're going to do. You're a guest at my wedding, that's all you are to me. But I do love my sisters and so, for appearances' sake, I'll be polite to you, but never, ever pretend that you love or care for me...'

'I do,' Anderson said, and he meant it. 'Now that I've got to know you.'

'Well, your timing's crap,' Naomi said. 'It's going to take a very long time to convince me. For now, I'll see you at the church.'

Sevastyan stood in the church next to Daniil.

'Nervous?' Daniil said.

'I'm curious to see the dress,' Sev said.

He doubted if she'd wear black, even if was her favourite colour. His bet was on brown, the colour of faded roses and the colour of her eyes.

He turned and saw Anderson Anderson coming up the aisle and taking a seat by Judy.

'God, I love that woman,' Sev said, as he realised Naomi had sent her father away.

He looked at his side of the church and saw a very pregnant Libby sitting with Rachel, her friend.

Anya had taken time off from the ballet she was preforming in and gave him a smile, which Sev returned.

Mariya was here, wearing the earrings he had bought for her, and her mother, Renata, was here too.

He smiled at Mariya, but not her mother. Sev just offered a nod of acknowledgement to her.

It still hurt but it hurt less and less.

And there too was Allem with Jamal, who had flown in from Dubai with their newborn just to share in this day.

That meant a lot.

Emmanuel was here.

But then again, Emmanuel had been everywhere—ensuring the wedding was perfect. God, was that guy efficient. He should have hired him years ago, Sev thought.

But then he'd never have met Naomi.

Sev had never thought that he'd be marrying in a church, let alone with people he cared for on the groom's side.

No, he wasn't nervous, at least not until he heard Daniil's always calm voice suddenly shocked.

'Bozhe moi!'

Oh, my God!

Sev looked towards the back of the church and saw a face he would recognise for ever, no matter his age, and watched a man trying to slip quietly into the back pew.

'Nikolai!'

Tradition forgotten, Sev simply left the altar and, along with Daniil they walked swiftly towards the friend they had thought lost for ever.

'You drowned…'

'No.' Nikolai shook his head.

'I don't understand…'

'Not now,' Nikolai said. 'Later. Today is about your wedding.' The music changed and people stood but Sev stood there, still stunned.

'I thought…' He had always thought it was his fault. That had he turned around that night, his friend might have changed his mind. It was too early to sink in that Nikolai was here in the flesh but finally he had the chance to apologise. 'I'm sorry I ignored you that night. I should have asked more…'

'*Nyet,*' Nikolai said. 'You have nothing to be sorry for. Go and get married.'

Naomi stood at the entrance to the church and saw that two had finally become three. Daniil must have found Roman, she thought as Sev looked over.

Yes, Sev knew that he should get back into his place but he wanted to share the news with Naomi and so, as Daniil led Nikolai to sit with his wife at the front, Sev walked over to his future wife.

'Nikolai is here.'

'Nikolai?' Naomi frowned. 'But I thought...'

And she looked at a man some considered had little emotion and saw tears of gratitude in his eyes, and knew she could put anyone who thought that right.

'I'm so happy for you,' Naomi said. 'How do you feel?'

'Relieved,' Sev admitted, and then he looked at Naomi properly.

Nikolai's presence was an extra gift,

Sev trusted himself even more now.

'You look...' He just held her hands and looked down.

Her dark hair was tied back as it had been on the day they'd met and the dress was white. It fitted like a glove and showed off her creamy bust, and she held a huge bunch of white roses.

They meant something now.

And these very flowers would one day lie faded between the pages of a book and she would cherish them for ever.

He smiled because, yes, white was for weddings and white really showed off those unseen stars.

The ring and Naomi.

And then she smiled, and showed him that she could indeed flirt because that smile told him they would be playing virgins tonight.

Sev then kissed the bride.

A thorough kiss that was so loaded with passion and promise that she almost dropped the bouquet.

'Dearly beloved….' the vicar said, and then coughed.

They stopped and only then did they remember where they were.

'Let's go and get married,' Sev said.

Naomi did not walk down the aisle alone, she walked hand in hand with Sev, both smiling.

Their vows were beautiful and heartfelt and again Sev got to kiss the bride.

At a more appropriate time.

Back at the hotel as husband and wife, her father toasted the bride and groom.

Naomi was very pleased she'd found the nerve to say what she had to Anderson when she saw her father checking his phone as Sev gave his response and toasted the bridesmaids.

Then Daniil gave his speech.

He thanked everyone and said all the right things, and then he thanked those who had come from afar and those that were not here, and then Daniil got to a part that had Naomi's heart rise in her throat.

'Sev looked out for all of us. He would try to halt an argument or tell us when to pull back. He would also read to us,' Daniil said. 'Remember, Sev? Sometimes it was a book on cooking that he had found, or gardening. One time a carer had left a sexy book…' And they all started to laugh as Daniil explained how the boys had kept getting him to read it again.

'And then there were fairy tales,' Daniil continued. 'We used to laugh at them—a black laughter, but we all hoped, I think.'

Naomi remembered what Sev had told her on the flight when he had admitted he had lied about not wanting a family. Her hand went into his as Daniil admitted he had felt the same.

'Who would have thought…?' Daniil started, but then halted, and as Naomi looked up she knew why. There could only be one reason that Libby was walking out during her husband's speech at a wedding.

Daniil's new family was about to get bigger.

Oh, there were so many happy endings today.

'Wrap it up, Daniil,' Sev suggested, given that there was somewhere else his friend needed to be.

'Naomi and Sevastyan!'

That was all that was needed to be said tonight.

Naomi had never thought that she could be so happy—dancing with Sev and surrounded by people she loved.

There were also the people she cared about but didn't necessarily love, but only because they had not loved her.

Sev did.

He told her so every day when he woke her and every night when they went to bed and she told him the same.

It had taken both their lifetimes so far to find out how it felt to be loved and to be the most important person in the other's world.

'Happy?' Sev checked, as they danced.

'Very.' Naomi nodded, though she was starting to wilt. She wanted to tell Sev what had happened between her and her father and of course to find out more about Nikolai.

'Can we go up?' Sev spoke into her ear.

'Up?' Naomi checked.

'To our suite?'

'It's not even ten o'clock.'

'I don't care what time it is,' Sev said. 'I'm done with other people.'

'You can't leave your own wedding at ten.'

'I can.' Sev shrugged. 'Everyone is having a good time. Jamal and Allem have gone up to settle the baby. Daniil and Libby are at the hospital. Your mother is drunk...'

He just reeled it off in his matter-of-fact way that made her smile.

And he was right.

It had been a blissful day and, no, they didn't need to stay.

'The only person I want to really speak with is Nikolai, but that can wait,' Sev said. 'I've a feeling that conversation might take some time. Anyway, he seems busy with...'

'Rachel,' Naomi filled in the name. 'She's Libby's friend.'

'Well, Rachel is taking exceptionally good care of him while her friend has her baby.'

She was!

'One more dance,' Naomi said, as the music changed to sexy and slow and Sev pulled her in.

'One more dance,' Sev agreed, and then he told her something he had found out today.

'You know Daniil said I read them an erotic book?'

She nodded.

'That's where I knew that word from—*"krasavitsa".*'

It really wasn't very fair to use the word he often did when he came when they were in the middle of the dance floor.

And it made her stomach pull in on itself when he told her then that he'd only ever said it to her.

'We're going to say goodbye now,' Sev said, and a little

frantically she nodded. 'Then we're going to get into that elevator.' And then, like some expert quizmaster, he hit the stopwatch. 'The honeymoon starts now.'

* * * * *

#3405 THE CONSEQUENCE HE MUST CLAIM
The Wrong Heirs
by Dani Collins

Sorcha finally gave in to her irresistible boss the night she resigned—but a car crash stole Cesar Montero's memories of their shared passion! When he discovers Sorcha's secret, Cesar's determined to claim his child and relive that white-hot night...

#3406 THE SHEIKH'S PREGNANT PRISONER
by Tara Pammi

Bound by honor, Sheikh Zafir's one indulgence was his whirlwind affair with Lauren. Upon finding out she's carrying his child, Zafir imprisons Lauren in his palace. His heir will *not* be illegitimate, so now he must make Lauren his wife!

#3407 ILLICIT NIGHT WITH THE GREEK
One Night With Consequences
by Susanna Carr

Convinced that troublemaker Jodie has come to Athens to jeopardize a business deal, Stergios Antoniou makes her his prisoner. Jodie finds herself a slave to their destructive desire once more, and she leaves his private island with more than just memories...

#3408 A DEAL SEALED BY PASSION
by Louise Fuller

When free-spirited Flora Golding stands in the way of Massimo Sforza's latest acquisition, the tycoon plans to seduce the antagonistic beauty to get his way. Only he hadn't counted on her passion undoing all his carefully laid plans...

REQUEST YOUR
FREE BOOKS!

HARLEQUIN

Presents®

2 FREE NOVELS PLUS
2 FREE GIFTS!

YES! Please send me 2 FREE Harlequin Presents® novels and my 2 FREE gifts (gifts are worth about $10). After receiving them, if I don't wish to receive any more books, I can return the shipping statement marked "cancel." If I don't cancel, I will receive 6 brand-new novels every month and be billed just $4.30 per book in the U.S. or $5.24 per book in Canada. That's a saving of at least 13% off the cover price! It's quite a bargain! Shipping and handling is just 50¢ per book in the U.S. and 75¢ per book in Canada.* I understand that accepting the 2 free books and gifts places me under no obligation to buy anything. I can always return a shipment and cancel at any time. Even if I never buy another book, the two free books and gifts are mine to keep forever.

106/306 HDN GHRP

Name _____
(PLEASE PRINT)

Address _____ Apt. # _____

City _____ State/Prov. _____ Zip/Postal Code _____

Signature (if under 18, a parent or guardian must sign)

Mail to the **Reader Service:**
IN U.S.A.: P.O. Box 1867, Buffalo, NY 14240-1867
IN CANADA: P.O. Box 609, Fort Erie, Ontario L2A 5X3

**Are you a current subscriber to Harlequin Presents® books
and want to receive the larger-print edition?
Call 1-800-873-8635 or visit www.ReaderService.com.**

* Terms and prices subject to change without notice. Prices do not include applicable taxes. Sales tax applicable in N.Y. Canadian residents will be charged applicable taxes. Offer not valid in Quebec. This offer is limited to one order per household. Not valid for current subscribers to Harlequin Presents books. All orders subject to credit approval. Credit or debit balances in a customer's account(s) may be offset by any other outstanding balance owed by or to the customer. Please allow 4 to 6 weeks for delivery. Offer available while quantities last.

Your Privacy—The Reader Service is committed to protecting your privacy. Our Privacy Policy is available online at www.ReaderService.com or upon request from the Reader Service.

We make a portion of our mailing list available to reputable third parties that offer products we believe may interest you. If you prefer that we not exchange your name with third parties, or if you wish to clarify or modify your communication preferences, please visit us at www.ReaderService.com/consumerchoice or write to us at Reader Service Preference Service, P.O. Box 9062, Buffalo, NY 14240-9062. Include your complete name and address.

HP15

Outspoken housekeeper Poppy Arnold is definitely not wife material, but Gaetano Leonetti must make her a convenient proposal to become CEO of his family's bank!

Read on for a sneak preview of
LEONETTI'S HOUSEKEEPER BRIDE,
a sensational new story from bestselling author
Lynne Graham.

"Your ultimate goal is becoming CEO of the Leonetti Bank, and marrying me will deliver that," Poppy said slowly, luminous green eyes skimming to his lean, darkly handsome features in wonderment.

"The bank is my life, it always has been," Gaetano admitted without apology. "Nothing gives me as much of a buzz as a profitable deal."

"If I were to agree to this…and I'm not saying I *am* agreeing," Poppy warned in a rush, "when would the marriage take place?"

"Next month. I have a lot of pressing business to tie up before I can take the kind of honeymoon which will be expected," Gaetano explained.

At that disconcerting reference to a honeymoon, a tension headache tightened in a band across Poppy's brow and she lifted her fingers to press against her forehead. "I'm very tired. I'll sleep on this and give you an answer in the morning."

Gaetano slid fluidly out of his seat and approached her. "But you already know the answer."

Poppy settled angry green eyes on his lean, strong face. "Don't try to railroad me," she warned him.

"You like what I do to you," Gaetano husked with blazing confidence, running a teasing forefinger down over her cheek to stroke it along the soft curve of her full lower lip.

Poppy stared up at him, momentarily lost in the tawny blaze of his hot stare. He wanted her and he was letting her see it. Her whole body seized up in response, her nipples prickling while that painful hollow ached at the heart of her. She tore her gaze from his.

"If you're not going to let me have you, sleep in one of the spare rooms tonight," Gaetano instructed.

"Spare room," Poppy said shakily, the only words she could get past her tight throat because it hurt her that she wanted to say yes so badly. She didn't want to be used "to scratch an itch," not her first time anyway. Surely someday somewhere some man would want her for more than that? Gaetano only wanted the release of sex and would probably not have wanted her at all had they not been forced into such proximity.

Gaetano let her reach the door. "If I marry you, I'll expect you to share my bed."

Don't miss
LEONETTI'S HOUSEKEEPER BRIDE
by Lynne Graham, available February 2016 wherever
Harlequin Presents® books and ebooks are sold.

www.Harlequin.com

HARLEQUIN Presents®

Michelle Smart introduces the final installment of her glittering trilogy *The Kalliakis Crown*, where a tale of royal rumours and undeniable passion leads to two very different worlds colliding!

Crown Prince Helios is bound to marry a princess, so the discovery of his secret lover, Amy Green, could shatter the Kingdom of Agon.

Amy has ended their affair—but everyone knows Helios is not a man to be denied! Legally, he must wed someone of pure royal blood. But will he do as duty commands, or risk his crown to marry his mistress?

Find out what happens next in:

HELIOS CROWNS HIS MISTRESS

February 2016

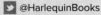

THE WORLD IS BETTER WITH

Romance

Harlequin has everything from contemporary, passionate and heartwarming to suspenseful and inspirational stories.

Whatever your mood, we have a romance just for you!